Accidental Mobster

Daisy Emory

TURBO KITTEN

Turbo Kitten Industries, PO Box 5012, Galt, CA 95632

www.TurboKittenIndustries.com

ACCIDENTAL Mobster

USA TODAY BESTSELLING AUTHOR *CATHERINE BANKS*
WRITING AS

DAISY EMORY

This book is dedicated to Erin. Thank you for always making me laugh and being a light in this often dark world. You are an amazing person and one of my precious friends. You are also the only person I am willing to share Vegeta with ;) Thank you for being my friend.

And, as always, thank you to my best friend and soulmate, Avery, for supporting me and being my rock.

Chapter One

Every Saturday at nine o'clock on the dot, two gorgeous men in suits entered my coffee shop, removed their sunglasses, and flashed me their dimples as they smiled.

They headed to the table by the window, removed their jackets, rolled up the sleeves of their shirts, and exposed gorgeously tanned, tattooed, and muscular forearms.

Before they started coming here, I'd had no idea that I had a thing for muscular forearms. Now, I was absolutely positive.

Yum. Yum. Double yum.

Since they came at the same time every Saturday, I already had their drinks made, still hot, and carried them over.

"Here you go, boys," I said, and set the drinks down in front of them.

Dane, the dark-haired, green-eyed hunk who sat on the left always drank a cappuccino with whipped cream and chocolate shavings.

Forrest, the brown-haired, blue-eyed brute who sat on the right drank black tea with a splash of milk and a dash of cinnamon. He hardly spoke, and today he winked at me.

I needed to buy an extra set of panties just for Saturdays.

"Let me know if you need—"

"Can we have two blueberry bagels with butter? Toasted?" Dane asked.

I nodded. "Right away."

Before anyone could ask me to do anything else, I rushed behind the counter and made their order, bringing them their plates with food still hot and butter still melting.

"I appreciate how quickly you get our orders, Amelia," Dane said. "You know you can make us wait."

I looked around the calm and collected café with all of the customers seated and asked, "Wait for what? There's no other customers waiting."

Forrest chuckled.

"Well, then how about you sit with us for a minute?" Dane asked.

After another look around to confirm my employees had everything under control, I removed my apron, grabbed a free chair, and sat at the end of their table.

"So, you own this place, right?" Dane asked.

I nodded. "Yep. Took a lot of jobs from thirteen until now to save up for it."

Dane and Forrest exchanged a look before Dane looked back at me.

"What town did you grow up in?" he asked.

Over the past few months, we'd had several conversations. They were all light topics, nothing serious, but they progressively got more personal. It was almost like they were trying to get to know me, but these two were far out of my league. So far out of my league I probably shouldn't have been allowed to talk to them.

"Little Logston about an hour away," I answered. Everyone knew the town. It was famous for being a farming community that provided all the produce for the large town of Pierceston, the largest town in the county.

"Why'd you choose to open in Pierceston?" Dane asked.

"Logston already has a café and I didn't want to take business from them since they've been there for three generations. Plus, I'm related to the Logston Café owners." I was related to half of Logston, but I didn't need to add that.

"So, you came to the big city to try to make it?" Dane asked, and took a bite of bagel.

I nodded. "Yep. I got tired of the small-town life and wanted to prove I could make it here."

"How are you doing so far?" he asked.

I flinched. I still wasn't in the black. Honestly, unless things picked up, I might have to look at closing within the year.

"It's been a little slow, but I'm hoping things will pick up soon," I said with a wide smile.

If my supplier would stop backing out on me last minute, forcing me to purchase the things I needed from out of town, I wouldn't be in the red.

They claimed another shop bought more than usual and they ended up not having enough for my order, but that excuse didn't hold up when they used it more than three times.

Forrest scowled. "What happened?"

He was always so intuitive.

"My supplier keeps getting bought out and I have to buy from a more expensive shop out of town," I admitted. "It's fine. I'll figure something out."

Forrest pulled out his phone and began typing into it quickly.

What was he doing?

"Be right back," he said, stood, and put his phone up to his ear as he walked out of the café.

"So, when you aren't here, checking on things, what do you do for fun?" Dane asked, sipping his drink.

"Honestly, I haven't been doing much," I answered with a shrug. Can't go out if you don't have money to spend. "I've mostly been playing video games or reading at home."

"You take off Saturday nights, right?" Dane asked.

How did he know that?

"Most times," I admitted with a nod.

"Then, are you free tonight?" he asked with a wide smile.

"Free for what?" I asked.

"A date," Dane said.

"You...me...date?" I asked, my eyes wide.

"Yes," he said with a chuckle, showing off his sexy dimples.

"What would we do on this date?" I asked.

"Well, there's going to be a festival. So, we could go to dinner and then walk around the festival, play some games, eat some dessert, shop at the booths, and things like that." Dane smiled.

It had been awhile since I'd been out on a date. And, Dane was smoking hot.

"What time?" I asked with a wide smile.

"I can pick you up at seven," he said. "Does that work?"

I nodded. That would give me enough time to go home, shower, debate what to wear for a few hours, make a dozen outfit changes, finally choose one, and make it back here. "Perfect. You can just pick me up here."

His lip twitched into a smirk, but then dropped back to a normal smile. "Great."

Forrest came back in, sat, and drank his tea.

"Everything good?" Dane asked him.

Forrest nodded. "Set in motion."

Dane nodded back. "Good."

"What do you two do for work?" I asked.

"We're assistants to a CEO," Dane answered.

"Assistants?" I asked. "Like get them their coffee and answer their phones?" I could not see these two as personal assistants.

Forrest shrugged. "Whatever the boss wants or needs us to do, we do it. Most times we go out and run errands for him."

"He must be a real big wig to need two assistants," I commented.

They both shrugged and took drinks.

Both of their phones made noises and they stood, grabbed their jackets, and their drinks.

"That's the boss sending us a task," Dane explained. "We set a specific tone so we would know."

I chuckled. "Smart."

He pulled a business card from his pocket and handed it to me. "I'll be here at seven, but here's my number so you have it on hand."

The card had his name and phone number on it. Nothing else.

Forrest handed me his card, which looked exactly the same. "You ever need anything, feel free to call us."

"Thanks," I whispered and stood as well.

They waved as they left and I waved back, dumbfounded by the interaction.

Shaking my head, I returned the chair I had used to the rightful table and cleaned up theirs before going to the back to get my stuff so I could go get ready for my date.

A date with Dane. It seemed surreal.

"You got everything you need for the rest of the day?" I asked Barbara, the current manager.

She looked up from the inventory sheet. "Yeah, but we are getting low on some items. I'll make you a list."

"How can we be getting low again? I just got an order in and we haven't been that busy," I said.

5

She shrugged. "I don't know what to tell you, but it seems like business is picking up, so maybe it's just picked up slow enough we hadn't noticed?"

"Well, that's a good thing," I said. "Just send me the list and I'll try to get a supplier."

She nodded and blew out a bubble of gum, let it pop, and said, "Sure thing, boss."

"I'm out for the rest of the day, so I'll leave it up to you," I told her and waved.

She waved. "Have a good one."

After a ten-minute drive home, a shower that involved way more shaving than I realized I needed, hair, makeup, and several hours debating between outfits, I made it back to the café with ten minutes to spare.

The café closed at four, so I parked in the back and doublechecked the doors were locked.

To my dismay, they were not locked and the back door was slightly ajar.

Maybe Barbara hadn't finished her nightly till and inventory counts?

Clutching my phone in one hand, I tiptoed inside, and to the back room.

The sound of something crashing and glass breaking had me rushing the rest of the way inside, hoping Barbara wasn't hurt.

Two men in ski masks looked up at me across a sea of my destroyed inventory.

"What are you doing?" I shrieked.

One of them raised a gun and I spun back towards the door, darting behind it just as the bullet hit above my head, going through the door and into the wall on the other side.

I yelped and ran outside, slamming the door closed behind me, and ran out onto the sidewalk.

"Amelia," Dane called out.

"Dane!" I screamed. "There's...there's..."

He ran to me, grabbed my upper arms, and asked, "What?"

"Café. Thieves. Guns. Shot at me," I gasped.

His eyes turned cold and he said, "Wait here."

I grabbed his wrist. "Don't. They'll kill you."

He had his phone out of his pocket and up to his ear. "Forrest. How far away are you? Someone tried to shoot her. They're in the café still. Hurry." He hung up, put his phone away, and patted my hand. "Forrest is almost—"

He didn't even get to finish his sentence before Forrest and another guy ran across the street. The other guy was even larger than Forrest.

"Inside?" Forrest asked.

I nodded.

Forrest nodded at the other guy and they marched towards the café's back door.

"They can't—"

Dane kept his hold on me. "Amelia, it's okay. They're not going to get killed. They're both ex-military and are trained for situations like this."

"Sh-shouldn't I call the cops?" I asked.

"Not yet," he said.

There were two gunshots and then Forrest stuck his head out and said, "Dane, come here."

I started to come, but Dane shook his head. "Just wait here."

I gnawed on my lip and obeyed.

Normally, I didn't like men ordering me around, but this was outside of my comfort zone.

Dane came out a few moments later and said, "They're just a couple of street junkies looking for some money or things to sell to buy some more drugs. Forrest and Shea will give them a stern talking to and let them go. Do you have a set of keys I can give Forrest to lock up with after he's done lecturing them?"

"You're just going to let them go? They destroyed my inventory. I was already running low and now I don't—"

"We'll cover it," Dane said. "They're actually from my old neighborhood, so I feel responsible."

"I can't let you do that," I said.

"We don't want them going to jail. If they do something like this again, we'll let the cops take them, but they deserve a second chance," he said.

I *was* all about second chances.

"Plus, if you call the cops and they come here, lights flashing, word will spread that the café isn't the safest place and you might lose business," he added. "I don't want you to lose business over these idiots. We can handle them."

"Okay," I agreed, and gave him the key to the door.

He smiled. "Great. Let me just go give this to Forrest and then we can go on our way. Forrest and Shea will get you the replacement supplies you need tonight."

I shook my head. "There's nothing available in the area. I've been calling all the suppliers for the past week and they've all been sold out."

"Just let us handle it. We've got some pull being assistants to our CEO, alright?"

He jogged back inside and I stared after him in disbelief.

Just who was their CEO? And why had Forrest and Shea been so close?

Those were questions I was determined to get an answer to later tonight.

Chapter Two

Dane took me to a beautiful restaurant that was way out of my price range. When he walked in, the hostess grabbed two menus and lead us to a table in a secluded part of the restaurant. A rose sat in a vase in the center. She bowed and hurried away before we could even say thank you.

I looked at the menu and gulped at the price tags.

"I recommend the steaks," Dane said. "They're the best in town."

Choosing a meal on a date always stressed me out. I closed my menu, set it on the table and asked, "Why don't you order for me? I'm not a picky eater and you've been here before, so I'll trust your judgment."

He smiled. "Okay. What about to drink?"

"I won't say no to a margarita," I said with a smirk.

He chuckled. "Salt or no salt?"

"No salt, please."

He set his menu down, and as if on command, a waiter walked over.

"Are you ready to order?" the waiter asked.

While Dane ordered, I took the time to admire his attire.

Earlier, I'd been preoccupied with someone trying to shoot me. Now, I could ogle his dark blue button-up shirt with the sleeves rolled up to his elbows. His black slacks weren't visible, but I had noticed those earlier. He'd spiked his hair and wore a very expensive watch.

Once the waiter left, he looked over at me and asked, "What?"

"Just wondering how large the wealth gap between us really is," I admitted. "Not that I'm intimidated by it, just curious."

"My employer pays me well, but it doesn't give me a lot of free time, so it is give-and-take. I only get one night off a week, sometimes not even that if he needs me for something," he explained. "I work more than twelve hours a day on average, too. He also provides me suits and the watch was a gift so that when his business partners see me, they see wealth and associate that with him as well, which helps him gain more partners. Sometimes, I wish I worked less, but most days I forget that I've already worked more than ten hours."

"That's crazy," I said.

He shrugged. "I enjoy it."

"So, you don't date often then?" I guessed.

He laughed. "No. Not often."

"That's why you're still single then? Can't find a woman who can handle you being gone that much?"

He wiped a drop of water from the outside of his glass and said, "That is one of the main issues. I'm sure you understand though, as an owner of your own business, how busy it can be."

I nodded. "I'm trying to let my manager take over more responsibilities, but..."

"It's hard to let go," he guessed.

I laughed and nodded. "Yeah."

"I get that," he said.

"So, how come Forrest and Shea were so close?" I asked, deciding it was better to get it all out now.

"We work just a block over," he said. "Saturdays the boss doesn't come in until ten, so we stop at the café for our morning drinks before going into work. They were outside for a quick walk, so they were even closer than usual."

Ah, that explained it.

"How come you don't come for coffee the other days?" I asked curiously. "Not that you have to exclusively buy your coffee from me, just wondering."

"We start work as early as six o'clock most other days and your café is sadly not open yet," he explained. "And we don't get breaks like most other assistants so we can't sneak out for coffee after we've already started."

"Your drinks," the waiter said and set them in front of us.

My margarita was huge and looked very tasty.

"Thank you," I said.

The waiter bowed and hurried away.

Another employee came over and set some bread and butter on our table without a word, just bowed and scurried off like he was afraid we would bite him.

"You come here a lot?" I asked, as I buttered a piece of bread for myself.

Dane nodded. "My boss loves their food, so we come here for business meetings often."

"Do you like your boss?" I asked.

"I love him. He's one of my best friends," he answered immediately.

I blinked in shock. Never had I met an assistant who loved their boss or was good friends with them.

"That's awesome," I said.

He chuckled. "Surprised you?"

"Well, yeah. Most people hate their bosses."

"You and my boss would probably get along great. Maybe one day I can introduce you," he said and buttered his own piece of bread.

"I'd like that," I said with a smile.

"If someone breaks in again, or attacks you, call me or Forrest, okay?" Dane said softly.

"I don't want you guys to get involved in a situation like that. What if you had gotten hurt? I should have just called the cops," I said softly.

"Do you have a security system?"

I shook my head. "I was going to get one, but the company came out, looked inside for ten minutes, and said that there was a problem and they had to get back to me. Then, they never did. I honestly forgot about it since I hadn't had any problems."

He scowled. "Have you had any other issues? Stock going missing or money going missing?"

"Stock has seemed like it's getting used up faster than it should, but we've also been getting more customers, so I'm not sure."

His phone chimed and he stood. "I'll be right back."

"Okay."

"Yeah?" he answered his phone as he walked away.

Not the most polite greeting, but if he knew who it was, I supposed I shouldn't judge him.

I indulged in another piece of bread and sipped on my margarita as I waited, but I didn't mind. Life as a business owner was usually not quiet and I respected that he helped his boss so much. If I could find an assistant like that it would make my life so much easier.

Not that I could afford to pay them...

Dane sat down with a smile. "Sorry for being gone so long. My boss wanted to remind me about an important event next Friday night."

"Well, I hope you remembered," I teased.

He chuckled. "It's the only thing he's been talking about for weeks. So, of course I remembered."

"What's your favorite music?" I asked.

He blinked a few times. "That's a sudden topic shift."

I shrugged. "I don't know how much time I'll have to get to know you, so I want to take advantage of the time I have."

"I don't have a favorite. I like everything except country," he answered. "You?"

"Everything except jazz," I said.

His jaw dropped. "You don't like jazz? You don't like saxophone?"

I cringed. "No, I hate the saxophone."

"I think this date is over," he teased.

I laughed. "Oh, are you a player?"

He shook his head. "No, but I love the sound."

"Well, you can put headphones on and listen," I offered.

He threw his head back and laughed.

My body warmed as I watched him laugh, a smile grew on my face on its own. He had a nice laugh. One that was warm and made all those nearby smile as well.

Our meal came and I had to resist moaning out loud as I enjoyed the deliciousness of the food. Everything was cooked to perfection and I was glad that I had asked him to order for me.

Once done, our dessert came and I had to wipe my mouth to keep the drool from falling on the tablecloth.

"This is seriously the best chocolate cake anywhere," Dane said.

I narrowed my eyes. "That sounds an awful lot like a challenge."

He smirked. "I would never in my lifetime dissuade someone from baking for me."

After we finished, we headed to the carnival. There were a

ton of people out, and I stayed close to his side to ensure we did not get separated.

"You alright?" he asked as we stopped in front of the game where you had to shoot the bottles over to win a prize.

"Crowds make me nervous sometimes," I admitted.

He put his arm around my waist and smiled down at me. "I'll keep you safe. Promise."

For some reason, I totally believed him.

"I think you deserve a memento of our evening," he said, and paid the carnie.

"Oh? You think you can win this rigged game?" I asked with a smirk.

He splayed his fingers out on my hip and said, "Yes." While staring down at me, he aimed the gun and shot four times in quick succession.

To my, and the carnie's, utter surprise, he shot down every single thing he had aimed at.

The carnie held out a large blue stuffed dog with shaky hands. "Congratulations, sir!"

"Thanks," Dane said, grabbed the dog, and held it out to me. "For my beautiful date."

"Thank you," I whispered and hugged it to my chest. The last time someone had won a prize for me was over two decades ago.

We played a few games against each other, but it became clear that he was much better than I was.

We got some funnel cake, drinks, and laughed until the carnival announced it was closing.

I walked with him back to my café, hugging my stuffed animal. "Thank you for my gift," I said softly.

He had his arm around my shoulders; the wind had chilled me enough that my shaking was noticeable, and he'd put his arm around me to keep me warm. "You are welcome. Thank you for agreeing to come out with me tonight. I hope you enjoyed yourself."

I nodded. "I definitely did."

We stopped at my car and I chewed on my lower lip. I hated this part of the night. Should I kiss him? Would he kiss me? Should I play hard to get?

"Next Friday, my boss is having a party," Dane said. "Would you come with me?"

"You want me to come meet your boss already?" I asked.

He nodded. "I need a date and I wouldn't want to go with anyone but you."

Meet his boss? A bigwig CEO who had a ton of money and was throwing a party that I likely would be shamed out of with my awful dress?

"Um, what type of party is it? I don't really have that many dresses for fancy occasions, since my life hasn't really called for it," I said.

He smiled. "I've got that covered."

"What?" I asked.

He leaned down slowly, giving me time to pull back, and kissed me lightly on the lips. "I'll text you, okay?"

I nodded. "Okay."

"Goodnight, Amelia."

"Goodnight, Dane."

He walked off into the night and I watched his perfect ass flex in his slacks as he walked away.

Okay, I could figure this out. I could find a dress that was appropriate to wear and I could totally spend an evening with a group of rich people despite having grown up on a farm.

Totally.

Right?

Chapter Three

True to their words, my replacement supplies arrived early Monday morning, and the suppliers I'd had so many issues with before were suddenly more than happy to help.

I decided it was time to distance myself even more from the cafe, and didn't go in for the entire week.

As Friday rolled around, I found a package on my doorstep with a bright red bow on it and a note from Dane that said: *Can't wait to see you.*

We had talked a bit over text, but our conversations had been more cordial than anything.

It wasn't too surprising that he didn't have time to chat if he was as busy as he had claimed and his boss was throwing a party.

What had surprised me was the number of messages I received from Forrest.

On Friday afternoon as I stared at my reflection, accusing it of trying to ruin me, he called.

"Hey, Forrest," I answered with a smile.

"You're coming tonight, right?" he asked.

"Of course," I said.

"Good," he answered. "I can't wait to see you."

My heart pounded. "Um, you know I'm coming as Dane's date, right?" I asked him.

He chuckled. "Yeah, I know. He won't stop rubbing it in. Don't worry, I'll take you out next weekend once this has calmed down."

He wanted to take me out?

"Did...did you just ask me out on a date?" I squeaked.

"Yeah. I'll take you out to the best Italian cuisine you've ever had. Nice little mom and pop joint," he said. "You'll love it."

"I'm sure I will. Won't Dane be mad you're trying to take me out behind his back?"

"It ain't behind his back if he knows, right?" Forrest asked. "In fact, he's right here glaring at me."

"It's alright, Amelia. We have an agreement that you can date us simultaneously," Dane said from the background of Forrest's call.

"Oh," I said, since there really wasn't anything else I could say to that statement.

"Anymore troubles at the café?" Forrest asked.

"No," I said. "Thank you for all your help that night. I really appreciated you risking your life for my stupid little shop."

"It's not a stupid shop," he said sincerely. "You make the best drinks in the city."

Was it stupid that his statement made me happy? Yes. Did that stop me? No.

"Thank you," I said softly. "I'm just glad the guys who broke in were such bad shots."

Forrest chuckled and I really enjoyed his deep laugh.

"Hey, let her go so she can finish getting ready," Dane said in the background.

"Dane and I will pick you up at eight, okay?" Forrest said.

"Okay," I agreed.

He hung up and I stared at the phone.

That had really happened, right?

I wasn't one prone to hallucinations, but I was seriously debating if the past week had really happened or not.

Once I was finished getting ready, I sat on my couch and twiddled my thumbs in nervous anticipation.

What was Dane and Forrest's boss really like? What if he was a total douche and I hated him?

Dane said he loved him and they were best friends, so I didn't want him to be a jerk or end up hating him.

What if he was even sexier than my two guys?

I laughed out loud at that thought. As if anyone was more attractive than them.

I studied my dress one more time, admiring the red, sparkly fabric that hugged my curves. The back and front were deep v-cuts, forcing me to go braless, thought thankfully that wasn't an issue for me. There were also slits on both sides of the dress that went up to my hip. It was the first dress with a slit up the sides that didn't force my legs out when I walked. I'd never had a dress with slits that only showed the slits when I stuck my leg out on purpose. It was glorious.

My phone chimed and I hurried out of my house to the waiting car, which turned out to be a limousine.

They had not said a limo would pick me up.

Dane and Forrest stepped out, dressed in tuxedos and looking fine as hell.

"Evening," I greeted them lamely.

"You look gorgeous," Dane said and kissed my cheek.

Forrest bowed and kissed the back of my hand. "Good evening, stunning."

"Um, hi," I said smartly.

That was me, conversationalist extraordinaire!

Forrest held open the door and I climbed inside. The limo

was much larger inside than I expected and I scooted towards the end of the seat, unsure where I was even supposed to sit.

Forrest and Dane took seats on the other two benches, smiling at me.

"Don't look so worried," Dane said. "You outshine any of the women who are going to show up."

Instead of scoffing like I wanted, I just smiled. "I'm glad you think so."

The driver took off and I leaned back in the seat, watching the scenery go by.

"Here," Forrest said and held out a glass of champagne.

I took it and he and Dane clinked their glasses against mine.

"To a night of fun," Dane said.

"Fun," I agreed with a smile.

We pulled up to a huge mansion that had a ton of paparazzi outside of it snapping pictures as they tried to catch a glimpse of anyone inside the limos that drove by.

"Don't worry, these limos are equipped with the darkest tints and the paparazzi won't be able to see anything," Dane said.

I honestly hadn't been worried about it, but for some reason, I relaxed a bit after he said that.

"Should I have eaten before I came?" I asked. "I didn't."

"Oh, there will be plenty of food available," Dane said. "Forrest and I spent two full days agonizing over the caterers' orders."

"Awesome," I whispered.

The car pulled up to the front and Forrest climbed out first, then Dane, and then as I stepped out, both held their hands out to assist me. I put my hand in both of theirs and let them both pull me out.

A few people snapped pictures, but I was too busy smiling up at the gorgeous men at my sides.

They both released my hands and I walked between them, feeling petite and special.

At the doorway, the person with the clipboard just nodded to them and we walked in.

Must be nice.

Inside, I realized that they were full of crap and ninety percent of the women there were freaking supermodels.

I recognized half the people there because they were either insanely rich business owners, or were actors or actresses.

"Whoa," I whispered.

"Come on," Dane said. "I've got to introduce you to our boss."

I let him and Forrest lead me inside.

Everyone knew them, calling out their names, some coming over to hug or kiss them on their cheeks.

At one point, they got pulled into a group of people and I stepped back to watch them interact.

"This tastes awful," a man said behind me.

I turned and found a man in an expensive suit glaring at a coffee machine.

"Maybe I can help," I offered.

He looked up from the pot, gave me a once over, and said, "If you're a guest, I couldn't possibly bother you."

He was quite possibly the most handsome man I had ever seen. He had a huge scar from his right temple to the top of his lip, and yet it did not take away how gorgeous he was. In fact, it added to it.

I smiled. "It's okay. I enjoy helping others." I walked over, opened the lid, and scoffed. "I bet it tastes like shit. There's twice as many grounds in here as there should be." My dress was short sleeved, so I didn't have to worry about ruining it as I scooped out the grounds and dumped them into the trashcan, then put half as many as there had been inside. I started the pot and as soon as the first cup was ready, the man took a drink and closed his eyes.

"Yes, perfection," he whispered as he drank. He opened his eyes and smiled. "I don't think we've met before."

I held out my hand. "Amelia," I introduced myself.

"Stephan," he said. "And did you come alone this evening?"

"No, sir, she came with us," Dane said behind me.

We turned and Forrest and Dane stood behind me.

Stephan's eyes widened. "Oh, this is the woman you've been prattling on about non-stop for months? I see your reputation stands."

"I, uh...what?"

"This is our boss," Dane explained. "Stephan Moriarty."

Stephan bowed. "It is a pleasure to meet you, Amelia. I've been trying to convince them to take you out and later introduce you to me for at least a month."

"Well, I'm glad you convinced them," I said, still incredibly dumbfounded.

"Is everything okay?" Forrest asked.

"The coffee was horrible, but Amelia has fixed it," Stephan said and winked at me.

"Oh, I didn't do anything," I said.

"Come, let's head to the main room," Stephan said. "I'd like to speak to you more, Amelia, but tonight may not be the best night for it. Dane. Forrest. Please be sure to show her a good time."

"Will do, sir," Forrest said with a nod.

"Yes, sir," Dane said.

"Good," Stephan said. He smiled wide. "We should all meet for lunch tomorrow."

"Um, sure," I agreed, still lost on what was happening.

We followed Stephan through the room, but he was stopped

by even more people than Dane and Forrest had been. Which did make sense, since this was his party after all.

"You look very uncertain," Dane whispered in my ear.

"I just realized where I have seen him before," I whispered. "I have a magazine with him on it."

Stephan Moriarty was one of the richest men in the world. He made billions in the technology fields, as well as other areas. He was also the most eligible bachelor in the country.

"I'm not surprised he likes you," Forrest said.

"Me neither," Dane said and smiled down at me. "I told you that you guys would get along."

"Dane. Forrest," Stephan called from a group he was standing in.

"Be right back," Dane said, and kissed my cheek before he and Forrest walked over to Stephan.

"Hello," a woman said behind me.

I turned and felt my eyes widen as I took in the beautiful model in a skin tight golden dress that gave a heavy view of her cleavage. She was one of my favorite models and I totally had a crush on her.

"Hi," I said, after looking around to make certain she was talking to me.

"I haven't seen you at one of these parties before. I'm Celia," she said and held out her hand.

"Amelia," I said and shook her hand.

"Are you a model?" she asked.

A bark of laughter escaped before I could stop it. "Uh, no. No, I'm not a model or an actress. I'm a nobody."

She tilted her head as she examined me. "Your dress is beautiful. A Cheron original, if I'm not mistaken, which I rarely am. If you're a nobody, how did you get such an exquisite and gorgeous dress?"

I looked down at my dress and felt my mouth go dry.

25

Cheron was a designer with a waitlist so long no regular person could hope to get on it. The designer sold dresses that started at six figures and they only allowed designers and millionaires to purchase from them.

"A Cheron?" I stroked a hand down the dress.

"You are an enigma. Who are you here with?" she asked and took a step closer to me. "If you're after Stephan, I'm going to warn you now to back off. I've been working on him for a long time, but someone as sweet and innocent as you shouldn't get involved with a man like that. You couldn't handle it."

A man like that?

"I'm not here with Stephan, but what is that supposed to mean?" I asked.

Dane stepped up beside me. "Everything alright here?"

I looked up at him and asked, "Is this a Cheron?"

His eyes widened as he looked down at me. He raised his gaze to Celia, glared, and asked, "What have you beautiful ladies been discussing?"

"Oh, I'm just trying to get to know her better," Celia said in a sickeningly sweet voice. "I know what it's like when you're the new girl on the block. I thought she might be a new model or actress I hadn't had the chance to meet yet."

"Definitely not either of those things," I said. "I've never been one who could handle strict diets."

"Oh, please," Celia said. "Your figure is banging."

"Well, you get a lot of muscle tone when you're moving haybales," I said with a shrug.

Her eyes widened and I wanted to slap myself on the forehead.

"Haybales?" she asked.

"Come on, it's almost time for the meal," Dane said, took my hand, and pulled me away from Celia.

"It was nice to meet you!" I called out to her.

She raised the champagne glass in her hand, and gave me a dazzling smile that wilted as soon as she turned away.

"Sorry, I'll try not to leave you alone again," Dane said.

"It's okay," I said. "I can handle a few conversations with people."

"She say anything cruel to you?" he asked.

I shrugged. "Not really. Aside from warning me not to try to go after Stephan." I laughed. "As if that was ever an option."

Dane looked down at me and frowned. "You're very self-deprecating. We'll have to work on that."

Once in the main room, we were all summoned for dinner at a massive table that sat at least fifty.

Dane pulled out my chair for me and pushed it in as I sat.

"Thank you for joining me on this joyous night," Stephan said, standing at the head of the table holding a glass filled with a dark liquid I assumed was whiskey. "Please, enjoy your evening and let us celebrate our friendships, no matter how new they might be." He looked at me as he raised his glass and I did the same, toasting along with everyone else.

Was it wrong of me to feel like his eyes were focused on me as we toasted?

It already felt wrong to have both Dane and Forrest focused on me, but what would they think if their boss had his attention on me as well?

I shook my head. No, that wasn't going to happen. I was totally overthinking it. He was probably just being nice because I was there with his assistants.

Waiters brought in food and I forgot about all my worries as I drooled over the succulent meal in front of us.

I ignored all proper protocol and devoured the food, having not even eaten lunch earlier.

So good!

When I finished, most of the other women hadn't even touched their food.

I dabbed at my lips and smiled coyly at Dane who just winked at me from across the table.

"Was the food to your liking?" Stephan asked me when we finally stood and people began to mingle again.

I nodded. "It was the best meal I've had in years."

"Well, if you liked that, I can't wait to hear what you think of dessert," he said and snapped his fingers.

Instantly, waiters hurried into the room with trays of wiggling chocolate pudding with whipped cream and a single red cherry atop them.

Stephan took two of the little bowls, handed me one, and said, "This is my favorite dessert."

"No pressure to like it then," I said with a smirk as I took it from him.

He chuckled and handed me a spoon from the next server who had a tray of them.

I took a bite and closed my eyes. Could you orgasm in your mouth? Because I was pretty certain I just had.

"It seems like you're enjoying that," Stephan commented.

I didn't need to look at him to know he was smiling.

"Try it with the whipped cream next," Dane whispered behind me.

My eyes flew open and I spun around, feeling like a terrible person for having been separated from my date, even if it had been by his boss, for a third time. "Uh, okay," I said, and did as he said.

Again, my eyes closed and I actually moaned out loud this time.

"See," Dane chuckled.

"Hey, what's going on over here without me?" Forrest asked, his tone full of teasing.

"I'm just food orgasming," I said, opened my eyes, and smiled up at the huge, delicious, man.

"Well, I definitely want to be here for this," he said with a smirk. A waiter brought Dane and Forrest their own cups and spoons.

"How often do you guys eat this dessert? I think it's highly unfair that you're all treating it like it's an ordinary dessert," I grumbled.

"It's my favorite, so I spoil them by having it at least twice a month," Stephan said.

"With a bit more cream and some cinnamon, I think I can make something better," I whispered to myself.

"Better?" Dane asked.

My eyes widened and I looked up at the three of them. "Um, sorry, that was supposed to be in my head."

"I would gladly challenge you to make something better. I will even provide a state-of-the-art kitchen with any ingredient you want," Stephan said. "As long as I get to taste it first."

Dane cleared his throat and Forrest folded his arms over his chest.

Stephan rolled his eyes. "Fine, as long as the three of us get to taste it."

"I would love to accept that challenge," I said.

"Tomorrow?" Stephan asked. "We could have lunch and then you could play in the kitchen."

Was Stephan Moriarty really asking me to have lunch and bake in his kitchen like we were friends? What was happening right now?

"Okay," I agreed with a wide smile.

Chapter Four

To ensure I didn't make an absolute idiot of myself, I limited my drinking to just two for the entire evening.

Everyone else did not have the same restraint, and it wasn't long before women were jumping into the pool in their six-figure dresses.

Dane and Forrest were pulled away by Stephan again. The three of them and another group of three men disappeared into a room where the doors were shut hard and two men stood outside of it, clearly to keep others out.

I stood outside, leaned against the side of the house, and watched the women splash each other.

"You're not going to join them?" a man asked beside me.

I turned my head. This man was just a few inches over my five foot six height, but he had broad shoulders that tapered to his waist, betraying how fit he was. What would he look like out of that tuxedo jacket? He also had gorgeous cerulean eyes framed by long, wavy black hair.

"No," I answered. "I don't want to ruin this dress."

I wasn't sure if Dane had rented it or borrowed it, but I was sure I wouldn't be able to keep it.

The man held out his hand. "I'm Arcadio. I work with Dane. He asked me to keep an eye on you while he had to help the boss with some business."

I shook his hand and chuckled. "So, Dane is a worrier? I wouldn't have thought that about him."

Arcadio put his hands behind his back and shrugged. "He just wanted to make sure nothing happened to you. You've made quite the impression on Forrest and Dane."

I felt my cheeks warm and looked back at the pool. "I think he's just worried because he knows this isn't my scene. Not that I have a scene, unless a farm or café count as a scene."

Dammit! Why did my mouth have to run away when I was nervous?

Arcadio chuckled. "Farms are much easier scenes to navigate than this. At least with farm animals you know their intentions. Humans are a lot harder to read."

I nodded. "True, but I had a few horses that would act like they were well behaved until they tried to knock you off using low-hanging tree branches."

Arcadio laughed again. "They sound like asses."

"They were," I agreed and chuckled. "Stubborn little jerks who took years of work to get them to stop trying to buck me off or knock me off at any chance. I've got a few scars from them and their shenanigans."

His eyes sparkled. "Oh?"

The dress had sleeves, but also a deep v on the back, so he could see my upper back and shoulder blades. I turned, showing him my back and said, "That crescent shaped scar on my left shoulder blade? That's from one of them slamming me into a jumping standard. It bled a ton and was so deep you could see my bone. Mama fainted and Dad had to stitch me up."

His fingertip traced the scar and I shivered. "Your dad stitched you up? Why didn't you go to a hospital?"

I turned back around and swallowed nervously, realizing that I needed to remember how to act properly. Had Dane come out and seen Arcadio touching my back like that, I doubted he would have been very happy.

Then again, I wasn't in a committed relationship with Dane or Forrest, so it wasn't awful of me to keep my options open. Right?

"We lived too far. The only other option was calling out the vet, but Tilly was rougher with humans and I didn't want her hurting me," I answered.

"Wow, you really are just a country bumpkin?" Celia asked. "I suppose that's why Dane got you that dress. How did you catch the eye of one of Moriarty's men?"

"Celia, you've had a lot to drink tonight," Arcadio said. "I think it's time for you to go home."

She rolled her eyes. "I'm fine."

"No, it's time for you to leave," Arcadio said.

"I haven't even had time to talk to Stephan," she pouted.

"I'll escort her out," a rumbling male voice said behind me.

A mountain of a man stepped out from behind me and I had to lean back to look up at him. It took me a moment to realize it was Shea, since I'd only caught a glimpse of him before he'd gone inside the café to deal with the intruders.

"Thanks," Arcadio said.

"Come on, Celia. I'll call you a car," he said, and then looked down at me and winked.

I shivered and dropped my head down. Why were there so many hot men in this place? Wait...were they all gay?

No, Dane and Forrest had expressed their interest in me and Dane had kissed me.

"Here," Arcadio said and draped his jacket around my shoulders.

He unbuttoned and rolled up the sleeves of his shirt. "I've been dying to get that thing off."

I had been right; he was really muscular.

"Well, I guess I'm happy to help then," I said with a smile.

He chuckled. "I appreciate it."

I looked at the open sliding glass doors and wondered how long Dane would be.

"If you're tired, there's a guest bedroom you can use to sleep in," Arcadio said. "It's in a part of the house that no visitors are allowed in."

"I'm a visitor," I reminded him.

He smirked. "You're Dane's date tonight, so you're part of the family."

Part of the family? That was a bit sudden, wasn't it?

"I'm okay," I said. "Thank you for the offer, though."

"Would you like to go inside and sit down? It can't be comfortable to stand in those heels."

It wasn't, but I hadn't wanted to complain.

I shrugged. "Sure."

"Just keep the jacket so I don't have to put it back on," he said.

I laughed and nodded. "Okay. Deal."

He led me back inside and to a living room where people were either making out, or in a large group, talking and laughing.

It felt like high school all over again, looking at the tables and groups and wondering where I would be allowed to sit.

Arcadio walked to a couple who were making out and kicked the man's shoe. "Head home," he ordered him.

The man stood and I recognized him as a new actor who became really popular after landing a role as a hero in a movie everyone talked about. "Okay," he said. The woman stood on shaky legs and the actor grabbed her hand and dragged her away.

Arcadio grumbled under his breath, brushed off the circular couch cushions, then waved me over.

I sat down, slid my heels off, and moaned softly.

He chuckled as he sat down across from me. "You're pretty good at hiding your discomfort."

I cringed as I rubbed my sore feet. "Well, all the other women were wearing theirs with stoic expressions, so I thought it was only fair I endured as well."

"You never have to endure for me," Dane said and sat beside me.

I smiled. "It's okay. I've been enjoying myself."

He leaned over and kissed my cheek. "I'm sorry I've been gone so long."

"I've kept her company," Arcadio said.

Dane took his jacket off, laid it on the back of the couch, loosened his tie, and rolled up the sleeves of his shirt.

He must have sensed my attention because he looked up and smirked.

I looked down at my feet again and resumed rubbing them, but winced when I hit a sore on the back of my heel.

"Be right back," Arcadio said and walked off.

Forrest sat on my other side, removed his jacket and tie, then grabbed one of my feet and started massaging it.

I gasped and then sighed as his large fingers found the exact spots that hurt.

"Here," Arcadio said.

I opened my eyes and fumbled to try to grab the band-aid from him, but Forrest had my foot in his massive hand and held it still as Arcadio put the band-aid on the back of my heel.

"You guys don't have—"

"Here," Shea said and held out a bottle of water to me.

I took it and felt like my entire face was on fire, my ears included. "Thanks."

Shea sat on Dane's other side, the couch completely full with the five of us on it.

Forrest and Arcadio fussed over my feet a bit and Arcadio added another band-aid to my other heel.

Having the full attention of four hot men was not something I'd expected tonight, but I was going to enjoy every blissful second of it.

Dane tugged on the jacket around my shoulders. "Whose is this?"

"Arcadio's," I answered without looking at him.

"He pawned it off on you so he could take it off? Typical," Dane teased.

"She was cold," Arcadio argued. "I was just being a gentleman."

I took it off and Arcadio scowled, but took it. "Thanks for letting me borrow it," I said quickly.

"You've got a lot of scars on your feet," Forrest commented.

"Lots of barefoot trips outside as a kid and teenager," I said. "Gravel is not kind to skin."

"What about these scars?" Dane asked and traced his finger over the top of my shoulder where my sleeve had gotten pushed up from Arcadio's jacket.

I glanced at the one's he touched. "One of those is from getting into a fight with a boar. He won. A couple I don't remember where I got them from. The crescent shaped one is from one of my horse's slamming me into a jumping standard to knock me off."

"What about this one?" Shea asked and leaned across Dane to touch the one on my chin.

"That one is embarrassing," I mumbled, not wanting to admit how I'd gotten in.

Dane held out his forearm and showed me a scar on the inside that looked like a jagged lightning bolt. "Jumped over a barbed wire fence and got caught on one of the pieces."

Shea took his jacket off, removed his tie, unbuttoned the top three buttons of his shirt, and pulled it to the side to show his chest. I glimpsed the top of a tattoo or two, but couldn't tell what they were. He showed me a gnarly rectangular shaped scar. "Got stabbed by an enemy when I was sweeping the house."

"So, you were in the military?" I asked. "Dane mentioned that when you went in after the guys who shot at me in my café."

"Someone shot at you?" Stephan asked as he grabbed a chair and dragged it over to join our circle.

All of the guys suddenly looked nervous and wouldn't meet my or Stephan's eyes.

"Um, yeah. Two guys broke into my café, trashed my inventory, and shot at me. Shea and Forrest apprehended them, though," I said.

Stephan narrowed his eyes at Shea. "Did they? And who were these men?"

"Junkies," Dane said and looked up, finally meeting Stephan's eyes. "Just a couple junkies from my old hometown."

Stephan leaned back in his chair, folded his arms across his chest, and asked, "Did you guys have a talk with them about righting their ways?"

"We did," Shea said. "They promised to get clean and won't bother Amelia ever again."

"I need to get a security system," I said. "I just need a better company than the last one, since they bailed on me for some reason."

"You've had a bit of trouble this year, haven't you?" Stephan asked.

I chuckled. "Yeah, but I'm hopeful it will work out. Thanks

to these guys I was able to get some stock in that I wasn't before."

"Oh?" Stephan asked.

Again, Dane and the others looked nervous.

"Why do I feel like I'm getting you guys in trouble?" I asked Dane softly.

He sighed, put his arm around my shoulders, and leaned his head against mine. "You totally are, but it's not your fault."

"That dress looks great on you," Shea said.

"Speaking of this dress..." I pulled away from Dane's arm, making him sit up straight. "Do you have clothes here I could change into, so I can give you this back?"

"Back?" Dane asked. "Why would you give it back?"

My mouth opened and closed twice before I finally said, "It's a Cheron!"

Stephan chuckled.

"That dress is yours," Dane said with a soft smile.

"This dress costs more than I could make in five years at the café. I can't accept this." I looked down at it and scowled. "Plus, this is probably the only time I'll ever get to wear it."

"Was my party not to your liking?" Stephan asked.

I looked up at him and frowned. "What?"

"You said you wouldn't have a chance to wear the dress again. Did you not enjoy the party tonight? Do you not want to come to another one?"

My mouth popped open in shock. "No! That's not what I meant at all! I enjoyed myself tonight and I would be honored if you asked me back again. I just didn't think—"

"Well, then you'll have another chance to wear it," Stephan said.

"I...I..." I was at a loss for words.

"If you want to change, I do have some clothes you can change into," Dane said. "If you want to be more comfortable."

"No, I'm fine. This dress is really comfortable," I said. Plus, I wanted to enjoy wearing it.

"Any issues tonight?" Stephan asked, leaning back and closing his eyes.

I looked around and realized everyone was gone. "When did everyone leave?" I asked.

"You nodded off," Forrest said.

"I did not," I replied indignantly. I would have remembered falling asleep.

"You did, too," Dane said. "While Forrest was rubbing your feet."

"No, my eyes were just closed because I was enjoying it," I grumbled.

"No major issues," Arcadio answered Stephan. "Although, Celia was being a bitch to Amelia."

"I escorted her out," Shea said in his rumbly voice.

"She threaten you?" Stephan asked without opening his eyes.

No one answered.

"Me?" I asked.

Stephan smirked. "Yes. I was asking you."

"She told me she's been working on you for a long time and warned me to back off," I admitted. "Told me I was too sweet and innocent and couldn't handle you."

"Oh? What did you say back?" Stephan asked, cracking one eye open.

"I didn't get a chance to respond because Dane came up at that point," I said with a shrug.

"Hm," Stephan said and closed his eye again.

I leaned back and Forrest grabbed the foot he hadn't massaged and started massaging it. "Mm," I said and closed my eyes. "You're very good at that."

"Glad to be of service," he said softly.

"Any leftovers?" Shea asked.

"Yeah. I think there's even a couple puddings left," Dane answered.

My eyes flew open and I asked, "Pudding?"

The men around me burst into laughter and my face burned.

I fell back and stared up at the ceiling. "I'm just going to die of embarrassment now."

Dane kissed my cheek and then Forrest kissed my other cheek.

"You're adorable. Please don't change," Stephan said. "We could use someone like you around more."

"If Celia heard you say that, she might throttle me," I said, and chuckled.

"Oh, she definitely would," Shea said. "But I'd toss her out before she could touch you."

"I think I've caused you guys more trouble than I'm worth," I said, my voice starting to trail off as my eyelids grew heavy. "I think Celia underestimated how much trouble I am and that *you* might not be able to handle *me*."

"Oh, we can handle you just fine, darlin'," Arcadio said.

"I love a challenge," Shea said.

"Tomorrow, I'm going to make you all the most delicious chocolate pudding dessert you have ever had," I said and yawned. "I might have to beat you off with a stick afterwards."

"Sweetheart, if I didn't have such tight leashes on them tonight, you would have had to start swinging as soon as you walked into the house," Stephan said.

I snorted. "Whatever."

Chapter Five

The sound of male laughter and conversation woke me. Blinking and wiping my eyes, I found myself in an unfamiliar room.

After a few seconds of terror, I remembered falling asleep on the couch with everyone. Then, vaguely, a memory of Shea carrying me to a room and Forrest tucking me in.

In horror, I realized I still wore the Cheron dress. I shrieked, fell out of the bed, and stripped the dress off, laying it flat on the sheets. It didn't look too bad, but I probably needed to get it professionally cleaned.

"What's wrong?" Dane asked as he burst into the room with Arcadio, Forrest, and Shea right behind them.

I turned, eyes wide, as all four got a completely unobstructed view of my naked body.

All four turned and Dane slammed the door shut behind them.

"Sorry!" he yelled from the other side of the door.

That's what I got for going commando in the dress, which I felt even worse about now that I knew it was a Cheron.

"It's fine," I said, and exhaled. "I woke up and realized you let me sleep in a dress that costs more than my house, and freaked out. I'll need to have it cleaned."

"There are some sweatpants, tank tops, and shirts in the drawers of the dresser in there," Forrest said. "We're almost done making breakfast."

"Okay," I said and started opening the drawers.

There were clothes, but they looked like they were all sized appropriately for Forrest.

The tank top at least fit and I was able to pull the sweatpants string tight and roll the waistband a few times to keep it in place. I put one of the t-shirts on, tying a knot in the back to make it fit better, and then fussed with my hair to try to get some of the tangles out.

I opened the door and found the hallway empty. "Is there a toothbrush or something I could use?" I called out.

"Door to your right," Arcadio called back.

I turned and walked into the most extravagant bathroom I had ever seen in my life. On the counter sat a toothbrush still in the package and a tube of travel sized toothpaste. On the opposite side of the counter was a hairbrush.

The fact that they had thought of this made me wonder how they were still single. I was fairly certain I was already in love.

Once I was freshened up, I journeyed through the mansion until I found the guys in the most perfect kitchen I had seen in my entire life.

My mouth hung open as I walked around, fingertips lightly touching all of the state-of-the-art equipment. Stephan hadn't been lying when he made the offer. There were gadgets I didn't even know what they did.

"Morning," Dane said and kissed my cheek.

I looked up at him and asked, "Do you guys live here?"

He nodded. "It makes things easier if we all live together.

That way the boss can ask us to do things, and doesn't have to wait a half hour or more for us to show up."

"I hope you like waffles," Forrest said as he walked by me carrying a huge plate of fluffy waffles. He kissed my cheek as he passed and I followed him out.

"I love waffles," I said. "I can't even remember the last time I had a Belgian waffle."

"They're my specialty," Forrest said confidently.

"Well, I can't wait to taste them." He led me to a different dining room than the one we had used last night and when I walked in, Shea, Arcadio, and Stephan stood.

"Morning," Stephan greeted. "I trust you slept well?"

I nodded. "Thank you for letting me crash here."

"Anytime," he said and winked.

"Here," Dane said and pulled out the chair between Shea and Arcadio.

I sat and he pushed my chair in, then walked around to take the seat on the opposite side of the table from me.

Once I sat, Shea, Arcadio, and Stephan sat, too. It wasn't often that I experienced men exemplifying etiquette like that.

The table had cut up fruits, scrambled eggs, bacon, butter, and syrup. My mouth watered and I started spooning out the strawberries and cantaloupe onto my plate first.

Forrest took the top waffle, set it on his plate, and then passed it to Dane on his left.

I stabbed a strawberry on my plate with my fork and put it in my mouth, instantly moaning. "These are the sweetest strawberries I've had in years. They taste like Mr. Starson's."

"They are from Starson Farms," Stephan said. "I have them delivered weekly. They are the sweetest around."

My mouth dropped. "How do you know about—"

"It's our job to find him the best produce for parties and functions," Dane said.

"When we did a search of the top-rated farms, Starson Farms was always the best rated. Plus, their prices are lower than most others, too," Forrest said.

I picked up another strawberry slice and bit it in half. "Their son is a tool, but the owners are very sweet."

"You know them personally?" Stephan asked as he buttered his waffle.

Shea handed me the plate of waffles and I waited until I had my waffle and gave the plate to Arcadio to answer.

"Yes."

It took me a full minute to butter my waffle because I had to be sure to get butter in every single indentation. Then, I poured the syrup in, also getting it into every indentation.

"Did you live there?" Stephan asked. "Are you from that town?"

Would he think less of me knowing I came from a small town? Would the others think less of me for it?

I nodded. "I was born and raised there. I only recently moved here to open my café. I didn't want to compete with the one that had been in the town for longer than I'd been alive."

"That's very commendable of you," Stephan said and smiled.

I shrugged. "My mama would have never forgiven me if I had opened one and caused her favorite place to close. Plus, I was tired of living in that little town."

There had been zero romantic prospects for me there. But if things didn't pick up here, I might have to go back.

"I rarely meet people with a kind soul," Stephan said. "You're very refreshing to be around."

That statement had me a bit uncertain, so I just said, "Thank you."

We all lapsed into silence as we ate, but it was companionable silence.

46

That silence was destroyed when I finally took a bite of Forrest's waffle and moaned loudly.

Every pair of eyes focused on me and my cheeks heated.

"Sorry," I said, embarrassed.

Forrest smiled. "Don't apologize. I'm glad you enjoy them."

"Did you put cinnamon in it?" I asked.

He smiled. "Just a dash."

"It's so good."

"Are you still up to the challenge of making a better dessert?" Stephan asked.

I nodded. "Definitely."

"You should have seen her face when she walked into the kitchen," Arcadio told him with a smirk. "Pure jealousy."

"It's the most perfect kitchen I've ever seen in my life," I said. "Of course I'm jealous."

"Do you bake your own pastries and other items that you sell at your café?" Arcadio asked.

"I used to, but one of the employees does it now. It just takes too much time and I'm trying to stop spending so much time there. I'd like it to run itself, well with the manager running it I mean."

"What are you going to do once it does run without you there?" Stephan asked and leaned his chin atop his clasped hands, elbows on the table.

I flushed, looked down at my plate, stabbed some eggs, and said, "Find a job I actually enjoy doing, even if it doesn't make much money, because the café will pay for my pretend, non-existent, never going to happen lifestyle."

"Such as painting, or what?" Shea asked.

"Honestly, I know it's a crazy dream. I just don't want to work in customer service forever. Maybe find a quiet desk job where I can file papers or something super mundane," I said.

"I'm sure I could find work as a receptionist. I'm really good at handling calendars and sorting mail."

"You want to be a receptionist...for fun?" Dane asked.

I shrugged. "It's easy enough."

"Try working for this guy and that will change your mind," Forrest muttered.

Normally, a boss would get mad that his employee was bad mouthing him to a person he had just met, but Stephan just laughed.

"I am pretty awful to deal with," Stephan admitted with a wide smile.

"Can I go play...I mean cook in your kitchen now?" I asked.

"Did she just ask to be excused from the table?" Arcadio whispered.

"Finally, someone with manners," Stephan said with a wearied sigh.

"Come on," Shea said beside me. "I'll help you find everything."

I stood and then remembered my manners and faced Stephan. "Thank you for sharing a meal with me." I faced Forrest. "Thank you for cooking me food." I spun and jogged after Shea, who had already taken off.

"You sure I can't keep her?" Stephan asked.

"No!" Forrest and Dane snapped.

Shea held open the door to the kitchen for me and followed me in. "The boss isn't going to stop teasing them about you."

I looked over my shoulder at him as I pulled out bowls I found beneath the island. "Why do you say that?"

"Well, those two were talking about you for a few weeks straight, so they set us up with pretty high expectations of you," Shea said.

I set the bowls down gently and said, "And then I came here and acted like a total small-town idiot."

Shea scowled. "What? No."

I sighed. "It's okay, Shea. I get it. After spending two minutes in that room full of models, millionaires, and actors, I knew I was out of my league here. At least you all were nice to me and I had fun."

The pot rack above the island was definitely built with six-foot-tall men in mind. I jumped and my fingertips touched the handle of the pot, but just made it sway back and forth. I grunted and jumped again, but had the same thing happen again. I put my knee up on the counter, but Shea grabbed my elbow and stopped me.

He grabbed the pot easily and set it on the counter.

I puffed out my cheeks in annoyance. "Thank you," I said.

He turned me around and twisted a chunk of my hair around his pointer finger. "You misunderstood what I was saying a minute ago, Amelia."

"You don't have to sugarcoat things, Shea. I'm a big girl. I understand when I don't fit in places," I said, and patted his hand.

"What the hell are you telling her?" Forrest asked as he walked into the kitchen. He stalked over to Shea with brows drawn into a furious scowl.

"It's okay," I said quickly and held my hands up to stop him. "He wasn't being rude."

"Like hell—" Forrest started, but Shea interrupted him.

"She misunderstood," Shea said. "I was—"

"Why is everyone yelling?" Dane asked as he walked in. He looked at me between Forrest and Shea and instantly rushed over. "What are you two doing? She's a guest."

"You guys are abnormally loud," Arcadio said as he came in.

I groaned and sat on the floor with my hands over my face. "I give up."

"Boys, why is my chef on the floor covering her face? Good dessert can't be made from the floor," Stephan said.

"She's not your chef," Arcadio, Shea, Forrest, and Dane snapped at the same time.

"You okay?" Arcadio asked while the others began to bicker, and set his hand on my shoulder.

"What am I doing here?" I asked. "I'm a poor, failing café owner. This is the home of one of the richest men in the country. I do not belong here."

"Failing?" Stephan asked.

I dropped my hands and looked up at the five men standing in the kitchen. "Yes. My business is failing. Distributors are refusing to work with me. People aren't coming. The first few months went fine and then something happened and they stopped. I'm probably going to have to just close it down and go back to my small town and help raise the horses again."

Raising horses wasn't that bad, but I despised shoveling manure. I could go back to the other jobs I'd had, but I was trying to avoid that.

"We took care of the distributors," Dane said. "You won't have problems with them anymore."

Arcadio wiped my cheeks and only then did I realize I was crying.

I stood and quickly wiped my face. "I'm sorry. This isn't your concern. I'll make you the dessert and then leave. My problems aren't yours and I don't want to bother you with them. I'll figure everything out on my own." Like I always did. "Shea, can you get me measuring cups, and spoons? Can someone else show me where the dry ingredients are stored?"

Everyone moved.

Shea got the measuring utensils.

Arcadio grabbed milk, eggs, and cream from the fridge.

Dane opened a door that I hadn't even seen and I followed

him into what was the pantry.

I pointed at the top where the cocoa powder was. While he jumped up to grab to the cocoa powder, I grabbed the sugar, cornstarch, salt, and other dry ingredients I needed.

When we came out of the pantry, I was excited to see all of the ingredients I needed on the island.

"Do you want us to stay here to help or leave?" Stephan asked. "I can order them all out of the room."

"You can stay, but no one else is allowed to help," I said as I washed my hands in the sink.

"Can we talk while you cook?" Arcadio asked.

I nodded. "I may only give you grunts in response to your comments or questions, but yes."

To my utter surprise, all of the men found spots on the counters out of my way and hopped on top of them.

Despite saying I would give grunts in response, I didn't even do that. I focused on my food and didn't look up until I finished cooking and putting everything in the dishes that Stephan had taken out for me.

I let it cool enough for them to eat before saying, "Done."

All of the men rushed over, grabbing one of the cups I had set out for them.

Holding my breath, I watched as they all spooned some out and into their mouths.

My hands clenched in front of my chest, my breathing stopped, and I froze, sure my heart even stopped.

All of the men tensed, froze, and then moaned.

"Okay, I was totally not expecting you to pull it off. This is definitely better," Stephan said.

"Oh my god, this is so good," Arcadio said. He looked up at me. "How are you still single?"

"Marry me?" Shea asked.

I didn't stop smiling for three days.

Chapter Six

True to their word, my distributors were suddenly very willing to work with me.

Knowing they had such pull made me nervous, but also super excited.

After a week of ensuring my café ran on its own, I finally stayed home the next week.

All four of the guys messaged me each day, chatting about their days or mine. They were quickly becoming my closest friends. Was it wrong to have super hot friends you wanted to sleep with?

Forrest and I scheduled a date for Saturday evening. I spent an hour figuring out my outfit.

He told me it was casual, but when I looked into his car and saw him in a suit, I was very nervous about my jeans and blouse.

"You look great," he said and kissed my cheek when I climbed into the car.

"You're in a suit." I bit my lip. "Do I need to change?"

He shook his head. "I had to go help the boss with something, so I had to put my suit on."

"You sure?" I asked.

He nodded. "Promise."

I put my seatbelt on and smoothed my shirt down. "So, where are we going?"

"Somewhere fun," he said with a twinkle in his eyes.

Now I was even more nervous for this date.

"Did everything go well for the café this week?" Forrest asked.

"Great. I think I can permanently step away," I said. "Though, I do need to find a job that will keep me busy that is fun."

"Oh? Have you started looking?" he asked.

I shook my head. "Nope. I thought I would start looking after I updated my resume."

Updating my resume was the worst thing I could think of doing.

I would put it off as long as I could...and maybe even longer. For now, I would take the time to get through my huge pile of books waiting for me to read them.

"Well, if you want some help, let me know," he said. "You could also add me as a reference."

"I don't think I'll need a reference for a filing job," I said, and laughed.

"It really boggles my mind that you would want such a boring job," he said. "I rushed to get out of those types of jobs."

"I had manual labor jobs as a kid, helping on farms and ranches. I considered jobs baking, but those would just ruin baking for me. Plus, I don't like being on my feet all day. Which is the main reason I won't do retail jobs. I just want something I can ghost through to get me through my days, earning a little bit of spending cash in case my business fails." I didn't want to admit it to him, but I didn't see the café lasting more than six more months. Even with the distributors working with me, unless business picked up soon, I would be forced to close my doors.

"Don't you have any hobbies, or wouldn't you rather just relax since you have the business running on its own now?" he asked. "I'd rather just watch movies or television than work."

"That gets boring after a while," I said. "I took off a few months, and after two weeks I was bored and begging my work to let me come back."

He laughed, glanced at me with a smirk, and said, "Sounds like you just didn't have the right company to spend your time with."

"My boyfriend was with me, but he just wanted to watch movies, which he fell asleep to ninety percent of the time, or play single player video games. Don't get me wrong, I love video games and watching him play was fun, but not hours straight each day," I said.

"What happened to this boyfriend?" he asked.

"We broke up shortly after that. Just too different and honestly, I didn't feel that spark or passion with him," I admitted.

"I bet he took you for granted and didn't romance you like he should have," he said.

I looked over at the large, muscular man, and asked, "Are you a romantic?"

He smirked. "Definitely. I love chick flicks, cheesy pick-up lines, and spend a lot of time buying presents that I know people will love."

"You just continue to surprise me," I said.

"Thank you. I hope to continue to surprise you as well," he said.

It wasn't until he pulled up the emergency break that I realized we had arrived for our date.

At a miniature golfing place that also had a building with

hundreds of arcade games. It was one of my favorite places, but I rarely got to go.

"You look excited. I chose well?" he asked.

I nodded vigorously. "Yes."

He climbed out of the car, removed his jacket, and tossed it into the backseat. I watched with rapt attention as he rolled his sleeves up, exposing his muscular forearms. I was a sucker for forearms.

"Are you going to get out?" he asked, a huge smile on his face.

Crap. I climbed out, wiped my mouth in case of drool, and followed him to the entrance.

"Just so you know, I'm not going to go easy on you," I told him. "Just because it's our first date means nothing when it comes to competitive games. In fact, let's make a bet."

His eyebrows rose. "A bet? I love betting, but I've always had really good luck when it comes to bets."

"Well, you go first then," I said, mainly because I wasn't sure what I wanted to bet yet. My mouth liked to get ahead of my brain often.

He paid, handed me a putter, then grabbed the two bright orange balls. "Well," he said thoughtfully.

I followed him into the miniature golfing course, well aware of all of the women looking in our direction. Strangely, there were several men looking at him, too, with expressions almost resembling fear. Was it because of his size? He was large, but why would they be scared?

"If I win, you have to cook me dinner, including dessert," he said.

Cooking someone I was dating dinner was one of my favorite things to do, so that really wasn't a prize, but I wasn't going to tell him that. "Okay. If I win, you have to sing *I'm a*

Little Teapot, shirtless, and let me record it." I'd totally thrown the shirtless part in there on a whim.

He threw his head back and laughed. When he dropped his head, his eyes seemed to glitter. "Oh, yes. I am definitely going to love making bets with you."

"Deal?" I asked and held out my hand.

He shook my hand and nodded. "Deal."

I took my golf ball from his hand, smiled wide, and headed to the first course. "Let the games begin."

Halfway through the course, my dreams of seeing him shirtless began to wilt. "How often do you play this?" I asked.

He shrugged one large shoulder and lined up his next putt. "Depends on what's going on with the boss. At least once every six months, though."

How had I not seen him here then?

"Do you come alone?" I asked.

He hit his putt and then looked at me. "I didn't take you for the jealous type."

I scoffed. "I'm not asking about you bringing other women. I wondered if you brought any of your coworkers." Although now I was curious if he had brought other women.

"Oh, trying to get intel to see if you can bet against the others, huh? Sneaky, sneaky woman." He laughed and stepped aside so I could make my putt. "I usually bring Shea with me."

My swing went wild, but somehow made it at least halfway to the hole. "You and Shea?" No wonder the men here looked afraid. If I saw both of them together and didn't know them, I'd be super intimidated.

"Why do you have that look on your face?" he asked, stepping close to me so he could whisper.

"I was just realizing why the men here look terrified of you. You and Shea together would be super intimidating if I didn't know you," I explained. Plus, it was sort of hilarious to picture the two huge men putting together, both bent over in half to reach the short height of the putters.

Watching him now was pretty comical. The putter looked too small for his large hands and he was stooped over comically.

"You judging me because I'm tall? You know I can't control my height. That's just rude," he said, but his smile betrayed how he really felt.

"So, what else do you do for fun?" I asked. "You guys said you don't get much time off, so you must only do things you really enjoy."

"Honestly, most nights and weekends we all just hang out with the boss at his place," he said and shrugged. "We have everything we could ever want or need there. He takes really good care of us."

It had to be nice to have someone there to take care of you, who cared about you, and not worry about your future. Not worry if you'll be lonely forever.

Warm arms wrapped around me in a hug and he whispered, "What's going on in your head right now?"

Crap. I'd gotten serious.

I stepped out of his arms, rubbed my face, and gave him my warmest smile. "That's really awesome that you have such a close relationship with your boss and that you guys can spend time together."

"It wasn't always like this, but with the boss expanding his terr...business, we've been able to have more luxuries," he said and beamed.

"Come on, we've got four more left and I'm not giving up yet!" I exclaimed and hit my ball into the hole.

When he lined up for the start of the next hole, I moved behind him and right when he swung, I fell into him, making his swing change. "Whoops," I said and darted back.

His ball veered right, but didn't go as far as I'd wanted it to.

He turned and narrowed his eyes. "You did that on purpose."

My mouth dropped and I held a hand to my chest. "I would never do such a thing."

He smiled and said, "Mm hm."

I put my ball down and lined up my shot. As expected, when I started to swing, he put his putter in the way. Since I had been expecting it, I stopped just before I hit my ball and turned to glare at him. "Excuse you."

He swung his putter up on to his shoulder and whistled, turned away, and pretended to be interested in the tiny stream that made this shot the most difficult. If you hit it wrong, it went right into the water.

I quickly made my putt and walked down the narrow concrete divider towards my ball. "I love the sound of flowing water." My foot slipped right as I stepped over the hole that went into the water.

My arms flailed and I squealed, sounding embarrassingly girly.

Forrest dropped his putter and grabbed me, holding me off the ground and saving my foot from the hole. "You really are klutzy."

"You can put me down," I said and patted his arm. "Thank you for saving me."

He held me and took the final few steps to my ball. "I think I like carrying you. Plus, you can't trip if I carry you."

"You're just showing off how strong you are," I said. "It's working."

He laughed and set me down.

I stood on tiptoe and brushed my lips across his. "Thanks."

He nodded and went to his ball, hitting it towards the hole.

At the final hole, we were only one stroke apart. This obstacle was the dreaded steep incline to a windmill that spun and had a little trap door that dropped. If you didn't hit it hard enough, you wouldn't make it up the ramp. If you timed it wrong you would hit either the windmill or the door. I almost always hit the stupid door.

"Final hole," he said and rocked on his feet. "Feeling nervous?"

I shook my head. "Nope. You?"

"I'm just trying to figure out what meal to ask you to make," he said, beaming already.

Not today, Satan...er...Forrest!

"Ladies first," I said and waved him forward.

He chuckled, lined his shot up, waited, and hit the ball. It rolled up the ramp and the door shut, making his ball fall back down.

"Nice try," I said and clapped. "Try again."

Another group stood behind us, waiting for their turn. They looked to be on a double date, all four about the same ages, and totally paired off.

Forrest rolled his eyes, knelt to grab his ball as it rolled to him, and lined it up again, taking even longer to watch the door and windmill. He hit and it went up and in.

Two hits.

"Not bad," I said and sauntered forward. If I hit this in one, I would win. With determination and focus, I watched the door and the windmill, waiting for the perfect time.

Someone behind Forrest sighed loudly. "Any day now, lady."

Forrest turned around. "Chill, boy. Let my girl take her time."

I looked back at the windmill, but my mind was focused on the fact that Forrest had just called me his.

"Oh, come on. Isn't she done yet?"

"She'll get there when she gets there."

"Dude I could have taken my shot three times by now."

I turned towards the guy to tell him to stop distracting me, but Forrest turned, looked at the woman with the guy, and said, "I'm sorry. You must go through a lot of batteries."

I doubled over in laughter, but didn't want to egg the guy on anymore, so I swung. The ball went in without hitting anything. I whooped, pumped my fist in the air, and danced around. "Oh, yeah. I won! I won. Woohoo. In your face!"

He laughed and said, "You won. Good job."

"About time," the rude guy muttered.

Forrest turned to yell at the guy, but I jumped up and kissed him, leaning my body weight against him so he had to wrap his arms around me or I would fall.

"Want to make another bet?" I asked.

He smiled down at me, arms still around me. "What are you betting this time?"

"If I win, you have to owe me one wish that I can redeem at any time," I said.

His smile wilted. "That's a steep bet."

Pulling out of his arms, I sauntered over to the barrels where we were supposed to return our putters, adding more sway to my hips to ensure I had his attention. I peeked over my shoulder and his eyes were focused on me. "If you're too afraid to take my bet, we can always leave."

"What are you betting you'll win on?" he asked and dropped his putter in the barrel.

"That I can get the most tickets in thirty minutes," I said with a wide smile.

"Make another bet," he said softly.

Why was he so against this bet? It was just a silly bet that I would use later for a kiss or something. Did he think I was going to ask for something crazy like a car?

"Did I hit a nerve or something?" I asked softly, I tugged on the hem of my shirt, and looked down at his shoes.

"I don't like owing people things," he said. "I didn't mean to make you feel bad."

"How about you owe me dinner if I win?" I asked, plastering a smile on my face before looking up at him. My feelings were hurt, but I didn't want to let it ruin the evening.

"She probably just needs a few drinks before going home with that asshole," the rude guy said as he put his putter in the barrel a few feet away from us.

This time, I didn't stop Forrest, not that I could have.

He turned, swung, and rude-y fell onto his butt, clutching his blood spurting nose.

A security guard came over, scowling, and I knew we were about to get tossed out. Forrest could even get arrested.

The security guard stopped and glared at the guy. "This punk bothering you, bro?"

Forrest nodded. "I gave him a few freebies, but he couldn't shut his mouth and insulted my girl."

"It's time for you four to leave," the security guard told them.

"What? But *he* punched *me*?" the guy yelled.

"Let's go inside and get tokens," Forrest said. He held his hand out to me and I set mine in it, still in shock that the security guard had been on his side.

"You didn't tell me what your bet is," I reminded him.

We stepped into the building and were assaulted by flashing lights, buzzers and other loud sounds, and laughter. It was a bit of a slap in the face, since outside was so quiet.

Forrest pulled his wallet out, grabbed a couple bills, and put them in the token machine. "If I win, you come work with us."

"Work...with you?"

He nodded. "Stephan already agreed and said you could have your choice of positions."

This was insane. There was no way he was serious.

I looked around, but no one seemed to be paying us any mind.

"What are you looking for?" he asked, gathered the tokens, and put them in a plastic cup they provided.

"For Shea or Dane to pop out and tell me you're joking," I said.

He smiled. "I'm serious. You can text Stephan and ask."

I rolled my eyes. "I don't have his number and even if I did, I wouldn't text him something like that."

"Want me to call him?" he asked and pulled his phone out.

"No!" I squeaked. "No. I believe you."

He put his phone away. "So, what do you say? Thirty minutes to get the most tickets."

"If I win, I get dinner. If you win, I come work with you at Stephan's billion dollar business."

He nodded. "Yep."

This was insane. Totally, certifiably, insane. If I didn't win, I could always quit. He hadn't put stipulations on how long I had to work there.

"Okay," I said and exhaled.

He held out his hand and we shook on it. "Let the games begin!" he shouted.

I spun and bolted across the arcade, dodging kids, teens, and grumpy parents. The game you could win the most tickets on was in a back corner and as luck would have it, completely empty. I was so winning this bet.

Chapter Seven

"I lost," I said for the tenth time, looking at my menu without really seeing it. "I can't believe I lost."

Forrest chuckled as he looked at his menu. "You totally lost."

We sat in a booth at a steakhouse back downtown.

Just like with Dane, the people knew Forrest and went out of their way to accommodate him. They were a reservation only restaurant, yet he walked in, no reservation, and we were seated within minutes.

"Order for me?" I requested with a smile.

He set his menu down and nodded. "Can do."

As soon as he set the menu down, a waiter rushed over with his pad and pen out. "What can I get for you, sir?"

Forrest ordered and I watched him. He talked confidently, but softly. Was it because his voice was deep and he could easily be accused of yelling if he talked in even a regular voice?

A few times during our arcade battle he had been near me and I'd taken the opportunity to watch him then, too. He smiled while he played the games, but then a man would come over to him, calling him "Bro" or something and his smile would disappear. He talked with the guys, but his shoulders were rigid and he didn't look at them.

"Would you like a drink?" Forrest asked me.

"A margarita, no salt, please," I requested.

The waiter bowed and hurried away.

"You guys aren't telling me something," I whispered. "I don't know what it is, but these people treat you differently, and I don't think it's just because Stephan is rich and you work for him."

Forrest leaned back in his chair and said, "I don't know what you mean."

"Why do guys keep calling you, 'bro?'"

He shrugged. "It's just a term for a guy you know. Like in California they say dude."

I did know that a lot of guys called each other bro, but it usually sounded different. When they called him bro it was like a term of respect.

My phone rang and I pulled it from my pocket. "Hello?"

"So, I hear you're going to be working with us starting Monday," Dane said.

My mouth dropped and I glared at Forrest. "You told Dane already?"

Forrest chuckled. "I told everyone already. You just have to pick your position."

"You don't even know what my skills are," I commented.

"Well, once we run your background we will," Dane said.

My entire body froze and felt like ice had been dumped on me.

"Oh? That's something you guys do, huh? I guess it makes sense. You wouldn't want possible saboteurs from competing companies coming in," I said, swallowing the panic down for later.

Forrest pulled his phone out and started typing away on it while scowling.

"Don't worry, the paperwork won't take that long to fill out and I'll help you," Dane said, completely oblivious to my fear.

"Well, I'm going to let you go so I can get back to my date with Forrest," I said and cleared my throat. Why did it feel so much tighter?

"Alright, babe, have fun," Dane said.

I put my phone in my pocket, using the time looking down to calm myself and put my date face back on.

"So?" I asked, looked up, and smiled. "What position do you think I should take?"

Forrest slid his phone into his pocket, put his elbows on the table, and leaned his chin on his hands. "Well, you wanted monotonous and boring, right? Mailroom would be a good job for that. Or data entry."

I nodded. "Right. Right."

"Do you like driving?" he asked.

"I mean..." I frowned. "...I don't *not* like driving. I don't go out for joy rides or anything, but I don't get angry driving in traffic or things like that."

"No road rage?" he asked.

I shook my head. "Nope. One of my mom's boyfriends had it bad, but I never get it."

"Well, I know Stephan is often looking for drivers," he said. "You could do that."

"I've never driven a limo before," I commented, finger tapping my chin. "It's probably like driving a tractor with a trailer behind it, making wide turns and such."

Forrest laughed softly. "You would be driving a car, not a limo."

"Who drives him now?" I asked. "I don't want to get anyone

fired just to get a job there. I can take an open position." Especially since I didn't plan on working there very long. Plus, how often did he need to be driven somewhere during the day? Weren't most CEOs in meetings half the day and responding to emails the other half?

"I usually drive him, but sometimes he sends me on other errands and has to ask someone else in the office to take him. If we had you assigned to him full time, that would take a huge load off my mind and his," he explained.

"What are the hours of this job?" I asked, narrowing my eyes.

"That all depends on the position you take. And you. It's not like I'm going to force you into a position to work swing shift or something," he said.

The waiter brought me my drink and a beer for Forrest.

We sipped our drinks silently while I thought about everything.

If he got all these perks working for Stephan, then I would get them, too. That wouldn't be so bad. I could get used to that. Maybe if I stayed for like, a month, I could still hold on to those perks even after I quit.

"How did you get so many tickets?" I asked. "I swear I only saw you play the types of games that give you low tickets even when you score high."

He smirked. "I'm not telling you. If I told you, you'd use it against me next time."

"Oh, you're pretty confident there's going to be a next time, are you?" I asked with a smirk.

He leaned forward and lowered his voice more. "I'm counting on it."

My pulse skyrocketed and I shifted in my seat. "Well, if we're going to be working together, you might get tired of me real quick."

Or realize how boring I am.

Our food came, interrupting him before he could respond.

The bowl before me held three of my favorite things: chicken, pasta, and cheese. The red pasta sauce was good, too, but I could take it or leave it.

After setting my napkin on my lap like a proper lady, I dug in, devouring half of it within minutes and stuffing myself into a food coma.

"Was it tasty? Or did you eat it too fast to enjoy?" Forrest asked, one corner of his lip curved upwards.

"That was the best chicken parmigiana I've ever had," I told him. "Now, I need a nap."

"I'm glad you liked it," he said. "I'll get them to box up your leftovers so you can enjoy them again tomorrow. Though, you might want to be sure you do it when you aren't going to need to go somewhere afterwards."

"Are we going somewhere afterwards?" I asked and sat up straighter.

"That's up to you. I was hoping you might come over tonight and spend some time at the house with us," he said.

Us. He meant Dane, Arcadio, and Shea.

Polyamory wasn't common, but my mom had been polyamorous, so I knew about it. So, I wasn't ashamed of my feelings for four guys at once. I was just afraid they wouldn't accept it.

"If they don't mind me crashing your man cave, I'd love to come over," I replied.

"Man cave?" he asked and shook his head. "I'd hardly call that place a man cave."

"Bachelor pad?" I asked.

He thought about it a moment and then nodded. "Yeah, that fits it better."

"Won't I cramp everyone's style? Being the only girl there?" I asked, but immediately realized I had no idea if I would be the only girl. Did they bring women back to the house often? Would it be like the party, just full of hot models everywhere?

"You make the best facial expressions," he said. "But I have no idea what they mean and can't even begin to decipher what you must be thinking about."

"That's probably for the best," I said with a wide smile. "Are you ready to blow this popsicle stand?"

Forrest throwing his head back and bellowing with laughter so loud it shook his entire body had not been the response I expected to that question.

Everyone in the restaurant turned to look at us, which had me slinking down in my chair and hiding my face.

"Why are you laughing so hard?" I asked.

He wiped tears from his cheeks. Tears. Actual tears.

"I'm sorry," he gasped. "I just haven't heard that phrase in so long and never on a date."

Yes, I was ridiculous and said weird things at times. He would have to get used to that if he wanted to continue dating me.

"I'm sorry," I said. "I didn't mean to offend you."

"Check," he called out, grabbed his napkin, and wiped his face. "Honey, you didn't offend me. You're far more worried about hurting my feelings than you should be."

The waiter dropped off our check and waited until Forrest handed him his credit card before running away again.

"Are you sure about me coming over? I don't want to cramp anyone's style." I set my napkin on the table to avoid looking directly at him.

"I'm positive," he said.

A different waiter grabbed our dishes and power walked to the kitchen.

Our check and to go containers arrived at the same time.

Forrest signed the bill, rushed to pull my chair out for me, then grabbed our containers.

As we walked out, I paid attention to the looks we were getting, not from the other customers, but the staff.

Worry. Possibly fear. Why?

I stayed silent all the way to the mansion, pondering all the things I had seen tonight.

We walked inside and I was relieved to see it was just the guys.

Forrest arched a brow. "Why do you look relieved?"

I chuckled nervously. "No reason. Hey, everyone."

They were sitting in the living room playing a video game on one of the many large, wall mounted TVs in the house. One of the characters died and the three of them turned to look at us.

Shea whistled. "Hey, beautiful. You're looking good tonight."

I looked down at my jeans and t-shirt with a scowl. "I'm not sure if that's sarcasm or just a terrible pick up line."

All four laughed.

Dane walked over and hugged me. "You always look good, babe."

Babe. When had we moved to that stage? Well, in text we had, but this was the first day he'd used it verbally.

"Thank you," I replied, and kissed his cheek.

"Are you here to play games?" Arcadio asked.

"I haven't played games in years," I admitted. "But I am totally up for beating your asses in some games."

"Oh ho!" Shea said with a wide smile. "The kitten has some claws."

I narrowed my eyes at him. "Kitten?"

He beamed, walked to stand before me, set his hand on my head, and then moved it horizontally until it hit his sternum. "You are tiny." He picked me up in a bridal carry against his

71

chest. "Light." I shoved at his chest and he set me down. "And feisty. You are a kitten."

"So, that makes you..." I pondered a word to use that would be fun without being super insulting.

"Ox," he said proudly.

"Uh..." Had he just called himself an ox?

"That's my nickname," he explained. "I'm Shea 'The Ox' Moseley."

"You're serious," I realized. I pointed at Forrest. "What's his name?"

"Forrest 'Flowers' Angrisani," Shea answered.

"F-flowers?" I stammered.

"I'm Dane 'Crackers' Cerino," Dane supplied.

"What about you?" I asked Arcadio.

He smiled, showing off his teeth. His canines were more pointed than most people's and always caught my attention. "Arcadio 'The Jackal' Mossa," he answered.

Ox. Flowers. Crackers. Jackal.

"Who the heck came up with your nicknames?" I asked.

"Me," Stephan answered behind me.

I spun, heart in my throat. "Oh, hi. I, um, didn't know you were here." Smacking my forehead after I said something would look stupid, but not thinking he would be in his own home was pretty stupid on its own.

"I didn't mean to startle you," he said softly.

"It's your house," I said. "Sorry if I'm intruding."

He put his hands in his pockets and the movement made me focus on his outfit. He was in a loose t-shirt with penguin pajama pants. "Intruding? Lovely, I told you that you're always welcome here. Plus, I hear you're going to be working for me soon. So, I need to get to know you better."

After a quick glare at Forrest, I looked at Stephan again. "About that. I know we made the bet for fun and all, so if you don't want me to work for you, I totally understand. Since I'm dating some of your employees, it might look—"

"I suggested they find a way to recruit you," Stephan said. "I have a feeling you're just the piece our puzzle is missing."

"That's one jagged puzzle," I whispered.

All five men burst into laughter.

Stephan shook his head. "I truly never expect the things you say. It is very refreshing. So, have you picked your position yet? Or would you prefer a tour first and then you can decide?"

"I suggested she become your driver," Forrest said. "Apparently she is immune to road rage."

"How did you come up with their nicknames?" I asked, trying desperately to change the subject.

"Those stories you have to earn," Stephan said with a smirk.

"Earn?" I asked, my mind instantly throwing itself into the gutter.

"She should work with me," Arcadio said. "I bet she would be a huge help."

Dane scoffed. "All you'd do is give her your work and then ogle her all day."

Arcadio shrugged. "If the work is getting done and my view improves, I see no downsides."

"She could work with me," Shea said. "We could be good cop, bad cop for anyone that we have to interrogate."

"Interrogate? What is your job?" I asked.

"Security," Shea replied.

"I think she should replace Forrest," Dane said. "I guarantee she'd be better at handling the calendar conflicts."

"You just want her to sit at the desk next to you," Forrest accused and folded his arms across his chest.

I looked around the room at all of these hot, rich men, and realized they were fighting over me working with them.

"You are all insane," I said softly.

All of them stopped talking and turned to look at me.

"How so?" Forrest asked.

"You have no idea if I can even use a computer," I reminded them.

They all rolled their eyes.

"You have a bachelor's degree," Dane said. "You can't get one without using a computer."

"How did you—" Had I told him I had a degree?

"It's on your wall at your place," Dane said with a chuckle.

"You've been in her place?" Arcadio asked. "Is it bright and cheery or plain and void of personal artifacts?"

"What is that supposed to—"

"I bet her room is the only place she has anything personal," Shea said.

They went back and forth a few times before I finally figured out how to change the topic.

"Why is everyone so scared of Forrest?" I asked loud enough they all heard me and stopped talking.

"What?" Stephan asked.

"Everywhere we went, people were scared of him. He punched a guy and the security guard threw the other guy out. Guys kept coming up to him and calling him 'bro,' and they let me into a ridiculously expensive restaurant in this outfit!" I waved at myself and realized I had ended up shouting at the end.

Apologizing would undermine what I wanted to know. So, I stood straight and waited for someone to respond.

"Why did you punch someone?" Dane asked.

"He was rude to Amelia multiple times," Forrest said. "I let him get away with it twice, but the third time I punched him. It was just a jab. I only broke his nose a little."

"A little?" I asked and my mouth hung open. "It was

spurting blood everywhere and made a disgusting crunching noise!" I yelled and waved my arms.

"You know the guy who insulted her?" Dane asked.

"Nope. Some young guy trying to show off for his girl," Forrest replied and shrugged.

"If you're going to ignore me, I might as well just go home," I said, folded my arms across my chest, and pouted.

Shea picked me up again and carried me to the couch. "Play games with us. It'll be fun, I promise."

"Is there any pudding?" I asked as I grabbed a controller. "I could totally go for some dessert."

Stephan chuckled. "I don't have any pudding left, sorry."

"I think we have some ice cream. I can make you a sundae," Arcadio offered.

"Oh, I haven't had a sundae in a while," I said.

Shea started the game before I could offer to go with Arcadio and Dane and Forrest sat on the couch with us.

"So, who wants to make a bet before we play?" I asked with a wide smile.

"She's devious. Don't let her fool you," Forrest warned them.

I beamed. "I haven't forgotten the bet you owe me. I intend to get it before I leave."

"What did you bet?" Dane asked and looked between Forrest and me.

"I'll show you the video afterwards," I promised.

Dane's eyes widened and I realized how that all sounded.

"No, nothing sexual. Geez Louise! What kind of girl do you take me for?" I rolled my eyes and looked at Shea. "Bet?"

"You beat me and I'll buy you a present," he said.

"A present? What kind of present?" I loved presents, but I hated surprises.

"It'll be a good one. Promise," he said. "If I win, you have to go on a date with me."

I glanced at Forrest and Dane, but neither seemed bothered by his request.

"Fine," I said.

He created a private lobby so we could fight each other in a one-on-one match. The game was a first-person shooter, but the characters had some super powers, too.

I adjusted my controls, then sat forward and focused. "Ready."

"Why do I feel like she's done this before?" Stephan asked behind me.

"She's a shark," Forrest said. "She beat me at miniature golf."

The timer counted down and then the match started.

My play should have been rusty, but it felt like riding a bike, and I beat Shea three to zero.

He set the controller down on the table, turned to face me fully, and asked, "Who are you?"

"Who's next?" I asked.

"Different game," Dane said and stood to look through the shelf beside the TV with the game cases.

"You don't actually have to get me a gift," I told Shea. "I just play better with bets."

"No, I owe you a gift. You won fair and square," he said and pulled out his phone.

"Do you need a ride Monday morning?" Stephan asked me.

"No, I'll drive," I said. "What time am I supposed to arrive? Do I need to bring anything? I haven't updated my resume yet."

"Just yourself and your driver's license for the background check," he said.

Again, my entire body froze and I struggled for a breath. "Can do," I replied as calmly as I could.

"Forrest, can I talk to you a second?" Stephan asked.

Arcadio set a sundae on the table with whipped cream and a beautiful red cherry on the top. I kissed his cheek, set the controller down, and picked it up. "Thank you!"

Shea stood and he and Dane whispered conspiratorially around the games, pointing at one and then another as they tried to decide.

I ate a bite of my ice cream and my eyes closed as I enjoyed the sweet strawberry ice cream with whipped cream, chocolate syrup, and sprinkles that had been hidden beneath the whipped cream. A tiny moan escaped. "So good."

"I'm glad you like strawberry. I was worried you wouldn't," Arcadio said.

I opened my eyes and looked around at the five men staring at me. "Why are you staring at me?"

"Do you always moan when you eat?" Shea asked.

My cheeks warmed and I looked down, scooping some more ice cream out. "Only when it's really good or something I haven't had in a while."

"We're going to have to make her eat bland things at work or we'll be fighting men off her with a club," Stephan commented.

I set the ice cream down, took my shoes off, and walked to the door to set them down.

Normally, I was pretty good about holding in my sounds, but I felt more relaxed around them than I did other people. Clearly, I needed to work on it, though.

"What is it about your past that you don't want us to find out?" Stephan asked me softly.

I raised my head and found him leaning against the wall across the hallway from me. "What?"

"You reacted negatively both times a background check was mentioned. Do you have a felony or something you don't want them to know about? If you tell me, I promise to keep it secret, as long as it doesn't affect them and won't cause any issues," he said.

I looked over at the guys, all of them now debating over which game to play next, and chewed on my lip. He was going to find out when he ran the background, so I might as well tell him. "It's kind of a long story. Can I tell you in your office or somewhere they won't hear?"

He nodded, turned, and said, "I'm stealing your girl for a minute."

All of them turned, eyes narrowed.

"What for?" Dane asked.

Stephan smiled, draped an arm around my shoulders, and said, "Business. Don't worry, she'll be back by the time you finally decide on what game she's going to beat you at."

He guided me down the hallway and to a huge office. It was wood paneled with a fireplace that took up almost one entire wall. It fit him. It also made me even more nervous. At least there weren't animal heads on the walls.

"Please, sit," Stephan said and waved at the leather chairs in front of his dark red mahogany desk.

I sat, put my hands in my lap, and drew a deep breath. I would do this and he would understand and everything would be fine. Right?

"So, Amelia, what is it about your past that you don't want them to know?" Stephan asked. He leaned back in his chair and looked completely at ease.

"I..." There wasn't really any easy way to say this, so I just had to do it like ripping off a band-aid. "I killed a man."

Chapter Eight

Stephan blinked at me. "Could you say that again?"

"There was this man who was obsessed with my mom. No matter how many times she told him she wasn't interested, he wouldn't leave her alone. My mom is polyamorous, so we always had at least one of her partners at the house with us. Well, they decided to go on a camping trip, just the boys, to bond more. While they were gone, that man came over and attacked my mom. I grabbed one of our guns, told him to leave, but he pulled out a pistol and aimed it at my mom. So, I shot him." The explanation tumbled out of me so fast, I wasn't sure if he even understood half of it.

He stared at me in silence for what felt like a full minute before he finally asked, "Did he kill your mom?"

I shook my head. "I killed him before he could pull the trigger." My body felt incredibly hot, a reaction to my anxiety and panic at telling the story again. I hated talking about it.

"So, it was self-defense," he said.

I nodded. "Yes, but it's still on my record because they arrested me initially." Sweat dripped down my spine and I shifted uncomfortably on the seat.

Daisy Emory

"Is that all?" he asked.

My mouth opened and closed as I stared at him in disbelief. Is that all? What did he mean? Killing someone, self-defense or not, was a serious thing.

"That's all," I answered after a moment. I needed to cool down. How?

He stood and smiled. "Well, that's nothing to be ashamed of, Amelia. You protected your mother. Trust me, those boys out there won't be put off by the fact that you protected your family and yourself. If you still don't want me to tell them, I won't, but I really don't think you need to hide it from them. I appreciate you being honest with me and I'll be sure to keep the truth of your background check secret from them."

I exhaled and felt my shoulders drop. I hadn't even realized how tense they were. "Thank you, Stephan."

He walked around, opened the door, and waved me out. "Let's return to the games."

I nodded, stood, and felt sweat all over my body. Cool. I needed something cool.

We walked out to the living room and all of the guys looked at me with varying expressions of worry and curiosity.

My face felt even hotter and I wondered if they had overheard. Had they eavesdropped while we were in the room?

I needed to cool off.

Pool! There was a pool outside.

"Excuse me for a moment," I said in a soft voice. My throat felt tight and it was hard to swallow. With quick steps, I walked outside, set my phone on one of the lounge chairs, and jumped into the pool.

Several of them called my name, the sound muffled by the water all around me.

Blessed cold relief. All of the anxiety leeched away and I felt a million times better.

I surfaced, drew in a huge breath, and smiled up at the five men staring down at me. "That felt amazing."

"You could have warned us," Forrest exhaled and squatted down at the edge of the pool. "I was getting ready to jump in after you."

Shea opened a door on the side of the house I hadn't seen and pulled out a towel. He set it on the lounge chair next to my phone.

I climbed out, wrapped the towel around myself, and sat on the chair. "Sorry to have startled you all. I just needed to cool off a bit."

All of them turned and looked at Stephan who held his hands up. "I didn't do anything. We just talked."

"Talking about my past makes me anxious," I explained. "Cold water helps me reset my brain."

"Come on, you can put some of the spare clothes on," Stephan said and held out his hand to me.

I took it and let him pull me up, smiling wide. "Thanks, boss."

With a skip to my step, I went to the room I had used last time, changed clothes, and went back out to the living room where they were all gathered. "Did you choose a game finally?" I asked, sat back in my spot, and resumed eating my sundae which was only a little melted.

On the table were three games. A racing game, a contemporary first-person shooter, and a side scrolling platform fighting game.

"We each want a chance to battle on these," Arcadio said.

"Everything okay?" Forrest asked softly, his mouth close to my ear.

I turned and gave him a peck on the lips. "Yes."

"We want you to choose your bets before we start playing," Dane said.

My eyes narrowed as I regarded all of them. "Do I get to know who I'm going to be battling? That's going to change what my bets are."

"Duh," Dane said with a smirk. "It wouldn't be fair if you didn't know what you were getting into."

I nodded. "Okay. I want to start with the racing game."

Shea walked out of the room and then returned with a piece of paper and a pen. "I'll write all the bets down so no one can try to wiggle their way out of them."

I smirked. "You going to write yours down so you don't forget?"

He smiled. "I already bought your present, Kitten. It will be here tomorrow."

My eyes widened and I fidgeted in my seat, desperately wanting to know what it was. "Do I get a hint?"

His smile widened. "You don't like surprises, do you?"

"No," I replied immediately. "I do not."

"Everyone likes getting surprise presents," Forrest argued.

"Yes, but not if I know they are coming and have to wait to find out what they are," I explained. "If you want to get me a surprise gift, just don't tell me. Wait until you have it in hand to give me, so I don't have to be anxious until I see it." I looked back at Shea. "It wasn't expensive, was it?"

His wide smile stayed in place as he remained silent.

Wonderful.

"Alright, if I win, you have to make me a dessert," Arcadio said.

What was I supposed to bet with these guys? I didn't want them all to get me presents. I also didn't want to ask for anything ludicrous. I would have asked for a favor at a later date, but the way Forrest had reacted made me wary of that option.

"If I win, you have to take me to the beach," I said, beaming since I finally figured something out.

Arcadio's eyebrows shot up. "The beach?"

I nodded. "I've never been."

"You've never been to the beach?" All five guys asked at once.

"No," I said.

"It's only two hours away," Stephan commented.

I shrugged.

"Okay, I accept the bet," Arcadio said.

"Great. Who is next?" I asked and rubbed my hands together. What else could I ask for?

"Me," Dane said. "If I win, you have to accept the dress I have for you."

"The Cheron?" I asked. That dress was already at my house, hanging in my closet in a garment bag so bugs and dust couldn't hurt it.

"The dress I have for you," he said again, smirking.

Did...did he have another dress?

"If I win you have to spend an entire evening with me, wearing only assless chaps, cowboy boots, and a cowboy hat," I said.

Shea let out a bark of laughter before covering his mouth. "Sorry."

"Babe, if you want to see me naked, all you have to do is ask," Dane said with a wink.

I rolled my eyes. "If you're too scared to accept the bet, I'll think of something softer."

"I accept," he said.

"If I win," Forrest began, "you have to delete the video I'm supposed to make for you."

"No way! That's totally not a fair bet. You might as well cancel our previous bet," I said. "If you want to go that route, then my bet would be to cancel the bet you won."

"Alright!" he said. "If I win, you have to spend an entire week here."

"Here?" I asked and looked at Stephan.

"It's our house, so they're allowed to have guests over," Stephan said.

Did they have women over often? Was I going to be just one of the other rotating girls for the month?

"Will there be other women staying here that week as well?" I asked.

"No, you will be the only person besides us here," Forrest said. "It would be just the six of us."

"If I win you have to make me breakfast in bed the next time we spend a night in the same house," I said.

"Deal," Forrest said with a nod.

"I'm next," Stephan said.

My eyes widened. "Y-you?"

He nodded. "You think I'm going to miss out on this fun? No way."

"Um, okay. What is your bet?" I asked. No way was I going to go first.

He tapped his chin as he looked at the ceiling in thought. "If I win, you have to sign a contract to work for me for a full year."

I narrowed my eyes. Did he know I planned to quit as soon as I could? How was he so intuitive?

"Do I still get to pick the position and work hours?" I asked. If I would be stuck working with him for a year, I needed to have some control over the situation.

He nodded. "We will negotiate position, hours, and income with everyone here present so you don't feel like I'm taking advantage of the situation."

Crap. That wasn't an awful deal. Honestly, this entire situation made me nervous. Why had they accepted me so quickly? Why were they all ready to have me work with them, spending eight hours a day in the same building, and allow me into their house? Shouldn't they be wary of strangers, not invite them in? What if I was psycho? There were plenty of people, men and women, who seemed great until you spent a lot of time with them and they couldn't hide how crazy they were.

"Okay. If I win, I get to quit after one month," I said and smiled victoriously.

"What?" Forrest asked.

"That's not a good deal," Dane grumbled.

"Don't accept that," Shea said.

"Sneaky woman," Arcadio mumbled beside me.

Stephan considered me a moment and then held his hand out. "Deal."

I shook his hand, picked up a controller, and said, "Let the games begin."

"I'm going to get us snacks and drinks since it's not my turn," Shea said.

"I'll come to help you carry things," Stephan said.

Arcadio picked up the second controller and started the racing game. "You're going to lose," he sang.

"We shall see," I said nonchalantly, but shifted forward on the couch, and prepared to try my hardest to beat him.

By the time Shea and Stephan returned, Arcadio was pouting on the floor, arms crossed over his chest, and mumbling about NPC interference.

"Are we going to play only these games?" I asked.

Forrest nodded. "Yeah."

"Cool," I said as I chose the character for the first-person shooter I was playing next. As soon as the game started, I grabbed the nearest pistol and snuck my way behind the boxes in the warehouse to find him.

"She knew right where a gun was," Dane commented. "She's definitely played this before."

Forrest poked his head up out of cover and I shot him with the pistol twice.

Dead.

"What the—" Dane exclaimed.

"Can you aim like that with a real gun?" Shea asked.

"In real life, I can use a gun, but I'm not a great aim," I answered as I reloaded in the game.

Forrest tried to rush me, but I shot him before he made it halfway across the warehouse.

"That was stupid," I said with a chuckle.

"I didn't think the pistol would be that good long distance in this game," Arcadio said softly.

"Pistols are often one of the best weapons in shooters," I replied.

This time, Forrest found a shotgun and snuck around to shoot me in the back. Unfortunately for him, I spawned right by him, pistol in hand, and killed him.

"I win! Mark that down, Shea!" I said with a wide smile.

"She isn't a shark," Forrest said. "She's a damn velociraptor."

"I do think I'm clever at times, thank you," I said and beamed.

Forrest handed the controller to Dane and said, "Good luck, man."

Dane sat beside me and said, "Same game."

I shrugged. "Okay."

Dane was a much better shot than me and much better at hiding. I lost within two minutes.

"What the heck?" I exclaimed. "Were you just pretending to be impressed by my shooting?"

He chuckled. "No, I was genuinely surprised by how good you are. I was worried I might not win, but I'm glad for all those nights playing."

I grabbed the drink Shea had brought me and took a big

gulp. Fiery sweetness slid down my throat and warmed my belly. "Fine. One loss. Who's next?"

"Me," Stephan said. "The final round is always the boss level."

I laughed at his joke and shook my head. "I bet you love making those jokes."

He sat beside me and said, "Mostly because those four groan and roll their eyes each time."

"So, platform fighting game?" I asked.

Stephan nodded. "Yes."

Side scrolling platform games were the ones I had grown up on. Mainly because we didn't have much money and I only had two games.

After each death, the scene changed to a new location, giving me time to take a drink or eat something.

We were tied two to two and the drink started to hit me.

Crapola. If I didn't win this point, I had to work for him for a year. My eyes were getting heavier by the second.

"Come on!" I shouted. "Time for me to win."

"Your cheeks are red. Are you feeling alright?" Stephan asked.

"Wonderful," I said, and then hiccupped. I covered my mouth and giggled. "Excuse me."

"Oh shit. She's drunk!" Arcadio exclaimed.

"Am not," I lied.

The round started and I jumped up to the third level to grab the ray gun. Stephan stayed at the bottom and grabbed the pistol.

I jumped down to the second level and Stephan jumped up to meet me.

The guys yelled around us, cheering for Stephan.

Angry that no one was rooting for me, I pulled the trigger.

Stephan jumped over the electric bolt from my ray gun and

shot me in the chest from point blank range. My character fell, the image flickered, and x's replaced the eyes.

Stephan had won.

Everyone cheered.

My eyes were glued to the screen, staring at "Player Two Wins" as I realized I had just lost a bet that required me to work for him for a full year.

"What have I done?" I whispered.

"I'm really looking forward to having you work for me," Stephan said.

I set my controller down and decided to get serious. "What if one or more of the guys end up not wanting to see me anymore?" I asked. "Do you expect me to work somewhere that I will feel uncomfortable? What if you decide I'm not good at the job I pick? Can you fire me? Or would you put me in a terrible position I'll hate since we have the deal?"

The guys looked around at each other, but didn't say anything.

"You realize that we went to your shop once a week for two months to see you, right?" Dane asked me softly.

"That doesn't change my questions at all. You guys don't know me that well. What if I'm psycho?"

"We've known plenty of psychos and you are not one of them," Forrest said.

"If you feel your mental or physical well being are in jeopardy, you may quit," Stephan said. "If one of these men decide that they don't want to see you anymore, they're morons and I'll have to send them to a different position until they find their brains."

I flopped back against the couch and sighed. "There's no way out of this. I totally made the wrong bed."

"If you decide you don't want to see these men anymore," Stephan continued, "you may tell me and I will either find you a position that will greatly limit any interactions with them, or we can discuss resignation."

"Fine," I groaned, my head swimming. "Forrest, can you take me home?"

"Do you just want to stay here?" Forrest asked. "You can use the same room."

I didn't want him to have to drive me so far to my house this late. It was past midnight already.

"Okay," I agreed. "That just means you have to make me breakfast in bed."

He smiled. "I'm okay with that."

With a groan, I stood.

My body swayed a bit and they all reached out towards me.

Shea scooped me up in the bridal carry again and said, "Let me carry you so you don't hurt yourself."

I leaned my head against his shoulder. "You're so warm and comfortable. Like a big teddy bear."

"I'll be your teddy bear anytime that you want," he whispered in my ear.

"Don't make promises you won't keep," I said and kissed his cheek. "It was Forrest's night, so I don't think he'd like you sleeping in the same bed as me."

"I don't think he'd mind," Shea said, "but I'm not going to push myself on you. I'll wait until you ask me to stay."

He set me on the bed and pulled the covers up to my shoulders. "Sleep well, Kitten," Shea whispered and kissed my cheek.

"Bye, Ox," I whispered and closed my eyes.

Chapter Nine

Halfway through the night, I woke screaming from a nightmare.

Forrest and Shea were the first in the room, Shea with a huge knife and Forrest with a handgun.

"Sorry. Nightmare," I said, panting with my heart racing.

Forrest lowered his gun and exhaled. "Scared ten years off my life, Amelia."

"Sorry," I said softly.

"You okay?" Shea asked.

I nodded, but the panic was still there. It was a dream I had often, a replay of the events from that night, but instead of me shooting him, he shot my mom and then me.

Shea left, but Forrest stayed, his brows pinched. "You sure you're okay?"

"Just a nightmare," I whispered.

He turned to leave and I called his name.

Without looking at him I asked, "Would you stay with me?" Being alone always made me feel worse.

"Okay, but keep your hands to yourself. I don't put out on the first date," he said and closed the door.

"We've been on two dates," I reminded him.

"Are you trying to seduce me?" He put the gun into the drawer in the dresser, climbed into the bed, and pushed me over gently so he could fit.

"No," I whispered. "Just stating facts."

"Everything okay?" Dane called through the door.

"Yeah," I called back.

"Night," he replied. His footsteps retreated down the hallway.

"Do you want me to hold you while you fall asleep?" Forrest asked.

"Please," I whispered.

He wrapped his large body around mine, spooning me, and slid his arm around my waist. "Do you want to talk about the nightmare?"

I shook my head vigorously.

"Okay," he whispered. "I won't let anyone hurt you, Amelia. I promise."

"Thank you," I whispered back, my heart no longer raced, and my breathing evened out quickly.

After breakfast, Arcadio drove me home. The others had some errand they had to run with Stephan.

"So, when do you want to go to the beach?" Arcadio asked.

"Whenever is convenient for you," I said. "I know you all are busier than I am."

"You okay?" he asked. "You've been quieter than usual this morning."

"Yeah," I replied and turned to smile at him. "I just haven't had my coffee yet."

We stopped at a red light and he turned to face me. "Will you go out with me Saturday?"

"On a date?" I asked.

He nodded.

"Have you all talked about this?" I asked. They were all good friends and I didn't want to do anything to ruin that.

"About you?" he asked.

I nodded. "About you all dating me?"

He nodded. The light turned green and he faced forward again. "We did, extensively. We all like you and agreed we wouldn't get jealous."

"It's really weird that you all let me into your lives so easily," I whispered. "Seriously, I could be a spy or something."

Arcadio chuckled. "Sweetheart, you suck at lying. There's no way you could be a spy or psycho. You would have exposed yourself already."

My mouth dropped. "I am a great liar!"

He shook his head. "You turn red when you lie."

I did? That was news to me. No wonder my mom never bought any of my lies when I was a kid.

"Fine, I suck at lying. That still doesn't explain it."

"We tried dating different women," he said, "but they usually ended up fighting each other or causing so much drama it wasn't worth it in the end. Dane and Forrest told us about you and we agreed to try more of a polyamorous relationship, but with you being our only girl. If you didn't mesh with one of us, we were going to call the whole thing off. Then, you walked in to the house in that dress, helped Stephan with the coffee, and stood up to that witch of a model. You are kind, hardworking, beautiful, and have one of the purest souls I've ever seen. Plus, you're silly and fun and when you're with us it feels like you filled a void we didn't realize was there. Even Stephan approves of you and he hates everyone."

"So, if we go out and think we don't mesh, everyone is going to call it off?" I asked.

He parked in front of my place and faced me. "It's not like that," he said. He reached over and took one of my hands in his. "I already know that we mesh, hon'. Now, we're just trying to build our relationships with you individually as well as together. We've all been texting you for weeks now. Trust me, we would know if our personalities didn't fit by now."

"You said I was beautiful," I whispered and smirked.

He leaned over, but stopped with his lips a breath from mine. "You are beautiful." His lips pressed against mine, but before I could try to return the kiss, he got out of the car.

We walked to my door and I asked, "Why are you guys trying to get me to work with you? Isn't it usually against policy for employees to date?"

"It's only against the rules if managers date the employees they manage," he said. "Since Stephan isn't dating you, it's fine."

"Is he gay?" I asked.

Arcadio shook his head. "No, he's asexual."

Well, that definitely explained it.

"Do you want to come in and watch a movie?" I asked. "I don't really have any plans the rest of the day?"

He pulled his phone out and checked his messages, then nodded. "Sure."

I pushed open the door and scowled. "I swore I locked this before I left."

Arcadio grabbed me and stopped me from entering. "Let me go in first, just in case."

"Okay." I wasn't going to argue.

He drew a handgun from an ankle holster and walked inside.

Did they all have guns?

A moment passed and another and he didn't come back.

I stepped inside cautiously. "Arcadio?" The entire living room was destroyed, all of my things tossed around and strewn about, even the couch cushions.

"Freeze," a deep voice ordered.

I froze, but turned to face the person.

A man I didn't recognize was standing over an unconscious Arcadio with a bat in his hand.

"Wh-who are you?" I asked.

"Where's your safe?" he asked.

"I don't have a safe," I replied. "This isn't the fifties."

"Where do you keep your valuables?" he asked. "You're dating the goons that work for Moriarty, so I know you've got some."

"I don't have anything," I said. "All my money is kept in my bank account and the only thing I have worth any money is a dress, which is in my closet."

"Bullshit!" the man yelled and took a step towards me, bat gripped in both hands. "You're just a filthy whore and a liar! Where are your jewels?"

Arcadio sat up silently behind the guy.

I needed to keep him distracted. "Look, man, I don't know what you've been told, but I don't have any jewelry, cash, or anything. You already searched my place, so you know that." I waved around at the disaster. "You would have found something by now."

Arcadio stood and pistol whipped the guy, knocking him out in one hit.

"Call Shea," Arcadio ordered me. "You have any duct tape or rope?"

"Shea? Shouldn't I call the cops?" I asked. My hands shook as I pulled my phone out and dialed Shea's number.

"Call Shea and then I'll call the cops. You're too shaken up," Arcadio said.

"Okay," I ran to my kitchen and grabbed the duct tape I kept under the sink. I threw it to Arcadio and he started taping the guy's hands together behind his back.

"Hey, Kitten. What's up?" Shea asked as he answered.

"There's a guy in my apartment. He ransacked it and was trying to get money or jewels," I said quickly. "Arcadio knocked him out and is tying him up, but he told me to call you before calling the cops."

"Are you hurt?" Shea asked. I heard the sound of squealing tires in the background of his call.

"No. He hit Arcadio in the head with the bat, though. Arcadio, are you okay?" I asked.

"He's fine," Shea said. "I'll be there in twenty minutes. Stay away from the guy and lock your door until I get there."

"Okay," I said. "I mean, the guy's not going to be able to do anything with the amount of duct tape Arcadio is using. And he only had a bat, so I don't think I'm in any danger."

"Please do it so I feel better?" he asked.

"Okay," I agreed. "Don't get a ticket."

He chuckled. "I won't."

I hung up and asked, "Are you okay?"

Arcadio nodded. "He hid behind the door and hit me pretty hard, but I'm fine. It's not even bleeding. Shea on the way?"

I nodded. "He said to lock the door and ordered me to stay away from the guy so I don't get hurt." Arcadio finished taping the guy's legs together at the ankles and the knees while we talked. "I don't think he's going to be doing anything."

He added a piece of tape to the guy's mouth and said, "No, he's not, but you should stay back, just in case. Hand me your phone first."

"You guys are overprotective, you know that?" I told him. I closed and locked the front door, handed Arcadio my phone, grabbed the couch cushions off the floor, and put them on the couch so I could sit down. "This is going to take me forever to clean," I grumbled. He'd broken all of my picture frames and taken the pictures out. He'd even torn apart some of my books.

That pissed me off the most. Why would he ruin my books? He could open them and see there was nothing there. He didn't have to tear them up. People had no respect for books. I wanted to kick him just for that.

"Pack your stuff," Arcadio told me.

I blinked at him. "What?"

"This place isn't safe for you, clearly. So, you're going to have to stay with us," he said.

I laughed, but realized he was serious. "I'm not going to live with you guys. I just have to keep my door locked and I'll be fine."

"He knew that you were dating us. If he knows, more people know. I'm not going to let you stay here, where you're not going to be safe," he said.

"Arcadio, I've only been dating any of you for two months. It is way too soon for me to move in with you," I argued.

"This isn't me asking you to move in because I want to move our relationship forward. This is me asking you to move in so that you don't get killed by some junkie or enemy of Stephan's," he argued back.

Moving in with five men when I was already going to start working with them full time for a year, seemed insane. I hadn't even gone on dates with Arcadio or Shea yet.

"At least pack a bag for the next couple of days," he said softly. "We can discuss it more when there isn't a guy on your floor surrounded by your destroyed property with our emotions running on high."

"What about the cops?" I asked. "We'll be stuck here for a few hours giving our reports and everything."

"I'll handle the cops," he said. "You just go in your room and pack a bag, okay?"

Someone knocked on the door and he waved at me.

"Fine," I said, stood, and tiptoed around the glass to my bedroom.

"Shut your door, too," Arcadio said.

"Overprotective," I called back, but obliged and shut the door.

Twice now someone had been in one of my places looking for valuables. This time did make more sense because I could totally understand someone thinking a woman dating one of those guys would have jewels or something in their place.

And I did feel afraid when I thought about staying here by myself, but living with them was...insane. Last night had been one of the best nights of sleep I'd had in years, so I couldn't lie and say that sharing a bed with Forrest hadn't been a pleasant experience.

Reluctantly, I packed the only suitcase I had with my clothes that were all over the floor. I would need to wash them when I got to their place and get rid of the glass pieces. I wanted to take some of my books, too, as well as the photos on the floor.

Once I was done packing, I started cleaning up my room. I put the drawers back in the dresser, fixed the bedding, and picked all the big pieces of glass up and tossed them in the tiny trash can I had in my room.

The last thing I picked up was the blue stuffed dog that Dane had won for me on our first date. The head was torn almost completely off and most of its stuffing was on the ground. Had he really thought something was going to be inside the dog?

There were two soft knocks on my door and then Shea opened it and peeked his head inside. "Hey."

"Hey," I replied and smiled up at him. "You didn't have to come, you know."

He scowled, walked over to me, and wrapped me up in a warm hug. "Yes, I did."

"Where is she?" Dane asked.

"This place is destroyed," Forrest grumbled.

"What are you all doing here?" I asked, my face still in Shea's chest. Tears welled in my eyes at both the realization that I might not be safe and that they had all come to check on me.

Shea released me and Dane pushed him to the side to wipe my cheeks. "We finished our errand and wanted to come check on you."

"I'm fine. He didn't even touch me," I said.

"Good," Dane said with a nod. He looked around and scowled. "I'm sorry your place is destroyed."

"I only care about the pictures and the books," I answered with a shrug. "And the dog."

Dane picked up the dog and said, "I'll have it fixed."

"I'll get the pictures," Forrest said. "I've got gloves so I won't cut myself."

"Did you pack?" Stephan asked from the doorway.

"I really don't think it's necessary for me to come live with you guys. I could get a hotel or something," I said.

He gave me an undecipherable look before saying, "No, you were put in danger because of your affiliation with me, so it is only fair that you stay with us. Besides, these four wouldn't be able to sleep at night thinking someone might hurt you."

"If you hadn't invited me to stay and watch a movie, I don't know what he might have done," Arcadio said, his fists clenched at his side and eyes on the floor.

"Where is he?" I asked with a scowl and looked around, but the taped-up man was nowhere to be seen.

"The cops picked him up already," Arcadio said.

"They didn't even ask me any questions," I muttered.

"Let's get you out of this mess," Stephan said and held his

hand out towards me. "The boys will clean up while I drive you back to the house."

"You're going to drive yourself?" I asked.

He chuckled. "I can drive myself when necessary and I think you might be in shock, darling."

That was a good possibility since I felt sort of numb now that I looked at my destroyed living room.

"Don't throw the books away," I whispered. "I'll need to replace the ones he tore."

"We'll make you a list and take good care of your things. I'll bring your pictures back with us," Forrest said.

"I'm going to come with you," Shea said. "I don't like the idea of you going by yourselves."

Stephan shrugged. "Suit yourself, Ox."

I tiptoed through the wreckage and took Stephan's still outstretched hand.

He led me down the stairs and at the bottom put his arm around my shoulders. "Don't worry, everything will be just fine. I'll let you pick your room when we get back and we can even discuss painting it or decorating it in any way you want."

"I don't like pink," I said.

"Good. I'm not a fan of it either," Stephan replied.

We walked by Arcadio's car and I swore I heard a thump in the trunk, but Stephan and Shea walked by unperturbed, so I had to have imagined it.

Chapter Ten

"What do you mean I can't wear jeans?" I asked with a scowl.

"Business casual means slacks," Stephan explained as we walked into the mansion. "No tennis shoes either."

"Fine," I said and let out an exasperated sigh. "I'll pick out an appropriate outfit once my clothes are washed."

"I'd prefer you get new clothes. You don't know if there are shards of glass in those," he said with a scowl.

He did have a point, but...

"I hate clothes shopping," I grumbled and plopped down on the couch.

"I can take you," Shea offered.

"It's not the company that bothers me, but picking out clothes, trying them on, paying way too much for one stupid shirt," I griped. "It is insane that I now have to pay over forty dollars for a single shirt. One shirt! I should learn to sew and make my own clothes." I knew full well that I couldn't make clothes. They'd look horrible, which is why I spent the money and bought clothes.

"You need clothes and you're not putting on clothes filled with glass," Shea said and folded his arms across his chest.

I fell sideways and laid on the couch with a groan. "This is not fair. First, some idiot breaks into my house because he thinks I have expensive things, which I don't. Then, I get ordered to move in here, and now I have to go clothes shopping. Worst. Day. Ever."

Okay, I was totally whining like a little, spoiled kid, but I was frustrated, tired, and cranky.

"Would you like a nap before we go shopping?" Shea asked.

I could hear the amusement in his voice and knew he was smirking. "Yes. And a blanket."

"I have a very soft and warm blanket," Shea said. "And a teddy bear you can use."

"A teddy bear?" Stephan asked.

"Me," Shea replied with a chuckle.

"I'm retreating to my study. If you need me, call, but I think you two can handle things on your own from here on," Stephan said. "Oh, and let her pick a room, Ox."

I listened to his retreating footsteps and closed my eyes. This was all so crazy.

Shea picked me up in a bridal carry and carried me to his room. He set me on the bed and I gasped at how soft the blanket was.

He kicked off his shoes, removed mine, and then sat on the edge of the bed.

I climbed up, laid my head on his pillow, and closed my eyes. "If Arcadio hadn't come in, I might have died," I whispered.

Shea reached out and set his hand on my calf. "That's why we want you to stay here. I would go on a murdering rampage to find the guy who hurt you and tear him into little tiny pieces."

"You're so sweet," I said, laughing.

"Go to sleep," he said. "I'll be nearby to ensure no one hurts you."

"I'm pretty sure no one would be stupid enough to come in here," I whispered.

"You'd be surprised," he grumbled.

"Do you have a gun, too?" I asked.

"What?" he asked me back.

"First Forrest had a gun and then Arcadio had one. I wondered if you had one, too."

"Does it bother you that they have guns?" he asked.

I shook my head as well as I could while lying down. "No. It just seems strange that you guys are carrying them around. Does Stephan get shot at a lot?"

"No, but he is a very wealthy man and as one of the top technology companies around, people do target him every now and then," he explained.

He said something else, but I fell asleep and didn't hear it.

By the time I woke up from my nap, everyone had returned home. When they heard I had to go clothes shopping, they all wanted to go. Stephan told them they could all go and he would just stay home.

So, the five of us climbed into one of their SUVs and we drove to the nearest shopping place. They tried to make me go to a designer brand store, but I reminded them I wasn't made of money as a small business owner and they reluctantly took me to the mall.

"The mall just isn't as safe," Arcadio said as we poured out of the SUV. His long hair was tied back in a ponytail that somehow made him look manlier and sexier.

"I'll be fast," I promised.

"You don't need to rush for us," Dane said.

"I'm not rushing for you. I'm rushing for me. The sooner we are out of here, the better."

This was the first time I'd been out with all four of them together. Shea and Forrest were the tallest, hovering behind me like mountains. Dane was a few inches shorter than Forrest, but with him walking ahead of me, he looked more like he was my height. Arcadio walked at my side, the closest to my height, but his broad shoulders, and scary scowl, ensured no one thought he was someone to be messed with.

All of them had changed into jeans. Dane and Arcadio had button-up shirts on, while Forrest and Shea had t-shirts on.

As we walked through the mall, women ogled them, some whispering to each other while they openly stared.

"You guys don't normally go out in a pack like this, do you?" I asked.

"No," Forrest answered. "We tend to draw a lot of attention when we're together."

"I see that," I said, and chuckled. The store I wanted to go into was just ahead, so I pointed at it. "That store."

"Dane," Shea said.

"On it," Dane said and walked faster.

"Uh, what's he on?" I asked.

"He's checking the store to make sure it's safe for you to go into," Shea answered.

"Oh my gosh, you guys are ridiculously protective. That's sweet and all, but how are you going to know if it's safe? There are going to be other shoppers around and you won't have any idea if they're dangerous or after me or not," I said. "Like, some little old lady could be carrying a knife in her purse and stab me or something."

"Been reading murder mysteries again?" Forrest asked behind me.

"No," I lied and pursed my lips in annoyance. I should not have let them handle my books.

"You had quite a few cheesy romance novels there," Arcadio said and turned to smirk at me.

"And?" I asked. "It's nice to dream about having a romance like that sometimes. I enjoy falling into the fantasy the books offer. I might never get to be a widow who meets her true love while vacationing in the Bahamas, but for that period of time that I'm reading...I am her. Most times, the real world is harsh and the books provide me an escape from it."

"I've never heard someone explain books like that before," Shea said softly. "That makes a lot of sense, though."

"Why would you want to be a widow?" Arcadio asked.

I rolled my eyes and shook my head. "That's what you got out of my explanation?"

"Clear," Dane said, and stepped out of the store in front of us.

"Good job," I said, and saluted him. I spun on my heel towards the store and marched inside with exaggerated steps.

"Smart ass," Dane grumbled behind me.

"Nice ass," I replied over my shoulder and winked at the four of them.

Quickly, I started grabbing clothes off the racks to try on. The guys spread out around the store, looking at the clothes, too. There weren't any other shoppers and the store employees stayed at the register, whispering and watching us.

"Going to try these on," I told Arcadio, since he was the closest to me and I didn't want to yell across the store.

He nodded and raised his left hand in the air.

I looked down at his right arm and narrowed my eyes at the clothes laid across it. "What are those?" I asked.

He smiled. "Clothes."

The fitting rooms had a curtain that separated them from

the rest of the store, and three couches sat in front of it. I'd seen many a defeated looking man sitting on those couches as they waited for their wives to try on their clothes and come out.

All four of the guys had clothes in their hands.

"Are you guys trying on clothes, too?" I asked.

They piled the clothes into my arms.

"Nope," Dane said, smiling wide and showing off his dimples. "You're going to try them on for us."

"Fashion show!" Arcadio said and sat on the couch with his hands behind his head and legs crossed at the ankles.

Oh, boy.

"You guys are ridiculous, but I'll humor you," I said. I looked at the sign on the door that said three item limit and scoffed. Clearly, they weren't enforcing that today.

All of the rooms were empty, so I chose the nearest one and dumped the clothes on the seat. It took me a minute to organize them on the provided hangers on the wall, but I finally got them sorted.

I put on the beige dress with a low bust line and slit on the side of the leg first. It was meant to look professional, but with how much cleavage it showed off, it was definitely not. I threw open the curtain and they either clapped or whistled.

"You are *not* wearing that to the office," Shea grumbled.

I walked over to him, leaned forward, and tugged on the front of his shirt. "Why not?"

He did an amazing job of keeping his eyes on my face. "Because I might get fired for throwing someone through a window when they do something to purposefully get an eyeful of that." He pointed at my chest, but still didn't look.

Damn, he had a lot of control right now. Arcadio sat beside him and stared openly.

"You should still buy it," Arcadio said.

I stood and rolled my eyes. "When would I wear this?"

"If Stephan has a function that requires us to look good and schmooze some people, that dress will be perfect," Forrest said.

I walked back into the fitting room, glancing back once to see if they appreciated this view, too.

Dane had his knuckle in his mouth and Arcadio beamed.

Good to know.

I traded the dress for a more practical pair of slacks and a blouse that I buttoned all the way up.

As soon as I stepped out, Arcadio booed.

Dane smacked Arcadio's arm. "It looks great," Dane said.

"Very professional," Shea said with a nod.

For thirty minutes, I put on a show for them, trying on all of the clothes they'd selected for me. I separated out the items I was going to buy for work, and left the rest on their hangers in the room.

All four scowled when they saw the ten items in my arms.

"Where's the rest?" Forrest asked.

"This is all I'm buying," I answered. "I just came to this store for work clothes. I'll get casual clothes at a different store."

Forrest and Arcadio stood and walked into the dressing room, bickering immediately.

"What are you two doing?" I called out, but they ignored me. With a sigh I said, "I'm going to go pay for this."

The two women and one man at the counter instantly slapped smiles on their faces when I approached.

One of the women stepped forward and touched a few buttons on the register. "Did you find everything you need, ma'am?"

I nodded. "Yes, thank you. And I'm sorry about them."

"Oh, it's quite alright. Let me ring these items up for you," she said.

I turned around to see what the guys were doing and heard

the man and woman still standing a bit behind the counter whispering to each other.

"She has to be dating Moriarty. Why else would his men be with her?" the woman said.

"You think he would let his men treat her like that? They were ogling her and openly drooling over her. Maybe she's a business allies' daughter or something?" he suggested.

"She's crazy to get mixed up with them. They're the most dangerous men in this city, no state," she whisper-hissed.

"You don't have to tell me. The people who have disappeared after offending Moriarty or attempting to ruin his business keeps piling up, but the police can't do anything about it because he has them in his pocket, too," he said.

"I hope she doesn't meet an early demise at their hands," she said and sighed. "Poor thing doesn't know what she's getting into."

Arcadio and Shea were arguing about something and Arcadio stuck his tongue out at the larger man. Shea grabbed Arcadio in a headlock and rubbed the top of Arcadio's head with his fist. The others laughed and Arcadio pulled free, smoothing his hair down while glaring at Shea.

They hardly looked like dangerous killers. They looked like friends having a good time. No, they had to be wrong about them.

The four men started to approach, all of them with clothes in their hands, so I turned back around.

The man and woman gave me wide smiles.

What did they mean about people disappearing? Were the guys and Stephan involved in shady business dealings? They were one of the biggest technology companies, but they didn't seem like bad people?

"Are you paying with card or cash?" the woman at the cash

register asked, finally done scanning and folding my items into bags.

"Card," I replied and pulled mine from my pocket to give to her.

"You alright?" Dane asked beside me.

I turned my head and looked up at him. "Yeah. I just don't like shopping, remember?"

He looked at the man and woman, who decided they needed to go in the back as quickly as possible.

"Here are your bags and your receipt," the woman said in front of me.

I took the bags and put the receipt inside one of them. I gave her my best smile and said, "Thank you for your help."

Stepping to the side, I watched as they each bought me more clothes.

"What are you four doing?" I asked with an exasperated sigh.

"We like these," Shea said. "So, we're getting them for you."

"Yeah, it's our fault your place got trashed," Forrest said. "It's only fair that we help rebuild your wardrobe."

"We should go to the lingerie store next," Dane said and winked at me.

"I am not putting on a lingerie show," I said and laughed. "You'd get us kicked out of the mall for sure."

"Nah, we'd be fine. But you're right, I don't want to chance other men standing around and watching the show, too," Dane said. "We'll just have to save that for later, in private."

I scoffed. "In your dreams, sir."

He bent forward. "Every night," he whispered, his breath against my ear made me shiver.

"You already got an advanced screening. You'll have to wait to earn the full show," I told him, spun, and walked out of the store.

They caught up to me quickly, once again surrounding me.

A couple guys approached and greeted Dane who walked at the head of us. The shortest said, "Hey, bro. Do you need anything?"

"Space," Dane said. "Go on."

They nodded and the other one said, "Sure thing, bro."

After a glance at me, they stopped and let us pass.

A shiver went down my spine and I took a step closer to Arcadio at my right.

"Don't worry about those guys," Arcadio said. "They do some work for us on occasion."

"What kind of work?" I asked.

He shrugged. "Random tasks."

The store I wanted to go to next came up and I pointed. "That one is the next and last store."

Dane went ahead and I scowled down at the floor.

Were those employees right? Was there more going on with Stephan and these guys than I thought? Had I gotten in over my head?

"Earth to Amelia," Forrest said in front of me.

I looked up and said, "Oh, sorry." I'd walked into the store without realizing it.

"Let me hold your bag," Shea offered.

After handing it off to him, I went quickly around the store, grabbing jeans, shirts, and other casual clothes that I needed for my evenings and time off work. This time, I didn't try them on, just took my pile to the counter and paid for them.

The guys must have noticed the shift in my attitude because they didn't say much, just helped me carry the additional bags that I had.

"Oh, I need shoes," I realized as we exited. "I guess one more store." Luckily, it was right next door.

Picking out shoes never took me long. We were in and out in fifteen minutes.

"You have got to be the fastest shopper I've ever met," Arcadio said with a chuckle.

"Efficiency is important," I said and winked at him. "At least when it comes to work."

"What about play?" Dane asked and skimmed his hand down my shoulder.

"Depends on the type of play," I replied and looked up at him from beneath my lashes. "I personally prefer when my partner takes his time to fully complete the game."

Their stunned silence made me realize what I had just said. I cursed myself for letting my flirtatiousness out. I tried so hard to hold it in.

"Sorry," I whispered and turned to head to the parking garage. "Ignore what I just said."

"Ignore it? That's the first time I've gotten you to finally spark back. Why would I ignore that?" Dane asked, coming up on my right side.

"We're just going back to the house now, right?" I asked.

"Need another nap?" Shea teased me.

"A shower," I said. "Oh. Do I need to buy toiletries while I'm here, too?" I probably needed at least tampons and stuff.

"We'll stop by a grocery store," Forrest replied. "I want to get some more snacks for the house anyway."

I nodded. "I'd like to get some of my own snacks, too. Plus, figure out what I'm going to take for lunches now that I'll be working again."

"You won't need to bring lunches. We either go out or order in," Arcadio said behind me.

"That's a lot of wasted money," I said and turned around so I could see them all. "You could save a ton of money if you made food and took it with you instead."

"Are you offering to make us lunches?" Dane asked. "I'll totally eat any lunch you make for me."

"Isn't there a kitchen in the building? Maybe we could just keep food there for her to cook there," Forrest suggested.

"I'm not cooking lunch every day," I said and rolled my eyes.

"So, you what, eat leftovers?" Shea asked.

I looked up at him, scowling. "Yeah?"

His nose scrunched up. "Ew."

My mouth dropped. "You don't eat leftovers?"

He shook his head. "No, that's gross."

I stopped in the middle of the walkway and stared, open mouthed, at the giant man. "You don't eat leftovers? Not even pizza or pasta?"

He shook his head. "They smell weird and have weird consistencies when they're reheated."

"You can't just heat everything up in a microwave," I said. "You use the oven to make crispy things crispy again. Pizza tastes best in the oven."

We resumed walking and I stayed silent as I mulled over the shock of him not eating anything that was reheated.

"So, what do you want to do this evening?" Shea asked.

I shrugged. "Whatever."

"Is everything okay?" Dane asked me softly.

I nodded. "Yeah."

"Did those employees say something to you?" he asked.

"No," I answered honestly. They hadn't said it *to me*.

"We could watch a movie," Arcadio suggested.

"Or play card games or something," Forrest added.

"I don't know many card games," I admitted. "Aside from Go Fish, of course."

"You've never gambled?" Dane asked.

I shook my head. When you didn't have much money, there was no point in gambling. It would just result in you losing the little money you did have. Plus, I had known a few men who ended up losing their houses and wives over gambling debts.

"We definitely need to teach you some card games," Arcadio said. "Stephan loves card games and it won't be much fun if you just sit them out all the time."

"I'm up for you teaching me," I said, and smiled at him.

He smirked. "I'm sure there are a few things I could teach you."

"Down, boy," I teased. "You and I haven't even been on a date yet."

"We'll fix that soon enough," he promised.

"So confident," I said. "All four of you are, actually. You guys might give me a complex."

"A complex?" Shea asked.

"Yeah. I mean, if one woman is enough to keep all of your attentions, she must be one hell of a woman."

"You definitely are," Dane said, and draped an arm around my shoulders. "So, how many dates do I need to take you on before I get that lingerie show?"

I let out a bark of laughter and shook my head. "Oh, Dane, you're too funny."

"Funny? I was being serious," he said.

"I'm hungry," Shea complained.

"You're always hungry," Forrest countered.

"Don't lie, you're hungry, too," Shea said.

"I didn't say I wasn't."

"I'm actually hungry, too," I admitted.

"We can pick out dinner at the store to cook at home," Arcadio said.

"Are you going to cook for me?" I asked.

He shrugged. "I cook sometimes."

"What's your favorite thing to cook?" I asked.

"I like cooking pasta dishes, but that's mainly because it's easy and I love pasta," he replied. "And my Nana loved making pasta dishes, so it was a staple in my life."

We finally made it out to the parking lot and climbed into the SUV. They tossed all my bags into the back before we headed to the grocery store.

The store we went to was close to the house and there weren't very many people inside. We decided to split up, but Shea opted to go with me.

"So, we know you were raised on a farm or ranch or whatever, but what did you do after you moved out?" Arcadio asked, while pulling bags of chips from the shelves and tossing them into the cart. We'd only made it down one aisle and the cart was already half full.

"Um, I went to college for a bit, worked some part-time jobs, had a boyfriend that didn't work out, and moved here to start my own business," I answered.

"What did you go to college for?" he asked me.

I shrugged. "It was just community college, and I didn't really have a major picked. It was just the general ed courses I took. Well, and a couple mythology and literature courses. School wasn't my favorite thing, though, and college was just a faster paced school, so I didn't last long."

"College was a lot of fun for me," he said. "I had Dane with me, though, and I'm pretty sure the only reason I had as much fun as I did was because of him."

"Oh, you've known each other that long?" I asked. My favorite chips were at the end of the aisle and I quickly added them to Arcadio's pile in the cart. Cheesy deliciousness.

"We've been friends since elementary school," he said. "All five of us."

"That must be nice," I said. "To have such close friends that you are still friends today and live with one another. It must be nice to know you can trust them and know you won't ever be lonely or anything."

He looked over at me with a scowl. "I never really thought about it like that, but yeah, it is nice not to worry about that." He was quiet a moment as we went down the next aisle – the cookie aisle – and I grabbed a few of my favorites. "Were you lonely, living in that place by yourself?"

How did I answer that? I mean, the answer was one hundred percent yes, but I didn't want them to feel bad for me. Eventually, I would have to move out on my own.

"At times, yes," I finally answered.

"So, you only had one boyfriend?" he asked, but turned to stare at the pasta shells so I couldn't see his face.

"Yeah. One boyfriend that I was with for about a year, but he and I just didn't mesh. I had a few dates, but hadn't really met anyone that I felt truly comfortable with," I answered.

"And you feel comfortable with us?" he asked.

"Yes," I replied immediately. "You guys make me feel safe and I feel a lot more relaxed around you than anyone else I've known. That's why sometimes I slip up and say things I probably shouldn't."

"What do you mean? You can say anything to us. We want you to feel comfortable," he said.

"We all still need to get to know each other better," I explained. "You guys don't really know me and I don't really know you, so I don't want to overstep boundaries."

"Boundaries? Like what?" he asked.

"Like making bets that make you guys uncomfortable," I said, and shrugged. "Things like that is what I mean."

"When did you do that?" he asked. "I don't remember anyone feeling uncomfortable about the bets we all made."

"Do you guys like lasagna?" I asked to change the subject. "I can make this ground beef pasta dish that tastes a lot like lasagna, but doesn't have the cheese in it."

"Sweetheart, we'll eat anything you make us. Most of us aren't picky eaters."

"Who is?" I asked. I grabbed a few different types of pasta shells and tossed them into the basket.

"Well, you know Shea doesn't like leftovers. Dane doesn't like eggplant. I'm not a huge fan of artichokes. I think that's probably it."

We went to the feminine hygiene aisle and I grabbed the supplies I would need, enough for two months at least since I wasn't sure how long they would want to keep me there. I knew eventually I would leave, but I wanted to be prepared, just in case.

We went to the frozen foods last and I got a few different flavors of ice cream. I missed having a treat at the end of the night.

"Anything else?" he asked.

Shea and Forrest turned down our aisle, each with a cart full of food.

"Fancy meeting you here," Forrest teased.

"I thought you guys were just getting snacks?" I asked, eyeing their huge assortment of food.

"We did," Shea replied.

"There you guys are," Dane said. He pushed a cart that was full of food, too.

"That is a ton of food, even for five guys," I commented.

"I mean, we only grabbed enough for the week," Shea said, and looked at his cart.

My mouth dropped. "You're joking, right?"

"No," they all answered simultaneously.

"You guys must waste a lot of food, don't you? There's no way you eat that much. That much food would last me at least two months," I said. Probably longer if I was good and rationed it out.

"You're a tiny kitten," Shea said with a smirk. "We eat a lot more than you do."

"How are you all not fat?" I would be huge if I ate even a quarter of the food they had.

"We work out a lot," Arcadio answered.

I glanced at his broad shoulders and realized in all this time, I'd never thought about them working out. "Do...do you have a gym at the mansion?" If they did, I was totally going to sneak down there to watch them work out.

"Duh," Shea said.

Oh, I was totally going to sneak in there. Could I install a camera? Would they notice if I put a nanny cam in? I bet I could sell pictures of them online to girls and earn a lot of money.

"You've got a devilish grin on your face that tells me your mind is in the gutter," Dane said.

I pretended to be shocked. "Me? Well, that's just rude. I was just wondering if you guys did circuit training or mainly did weight lifting." I mean, that was partly true.

"We do all of it," Dane answered. "We also do different types of martial arts training."

"Really?" I asked, a bit blindsided by that statement.

They all nodded.

"We'll have to start teaching you, too," Forrest said. "The sooner you can take care of yourself, the better we will all feel."

I wasn't going to argue because honestly, I felt the same way.

Chapter Eleven

With my driver's license in hand, I walked beside Shea into the high rise building that Stephan owned.

Shea had opted to stay home with me and walk me in for my first day, so I could bypass some of the security protocols they usually made new employees go through. No one at the security desk even questioned him as he grabbed a visitor sticker for me, slapped it on my shoulder, and waved me through the metal detectors.

Shea walked around the metal detectors and then took me to the elevators that would take us up to Stephan's office.

Everyone wore expensive outfits, had styled hair, and moved with purpose.

Everyone except me. I gawked at all of the shiny surfaces, chrome detailing, and beautiful opal and grey marble floors.

"This is the most beautiful building I have ever seen," I whispered to Shea.

He chuckled. "Tell Stephan that. He likes bragging about how much time and effort he put into making this building pretty."

"So, Mr. Security, what should I expect from here?" I asked.

"I'm going to take you to human resources, where they will give you a packet of papers to fill out. Then we go to Stephan's so you can talk and discuss what position you want. If you want a tour, then I'll give you a tour of the building and describe every area and what they do. You can observe them for a bit, or we will continue on until you finally have the full tour. Once that is done, we'll return to Stephan's office for you to finally choose your position. After that, you'll fill out your paperwork, get your ID card, go back to HR, and officially become one of the employee's here."

"Oh, is that all?" I asked with a chuckle.

"Well, after that is lunch, meetings, and I'm not sure what else Stephan has planned for the day," he answered.

"Can I take a nap first? I'm tired just from hearing all of that," I said and sighed.

Shea bent and kissed my cheek. "Kitten, we're right here with you. You'll be fine."

I didn't want to admit to him how much better that made me feel.

The elevator doors opened to a floor full of cubicles, with employees typing away on the computers.

Shea stepped out and I followed him to the third row, seventh cubicle down.

The woman in the cubicle had dozens of pictures of children on her cubicle wall, a short A-line haircut, and she wore a bright pink dress.

Shea cleared his throat.

She spun her chair around to look at us and smiled. "Hello, Shea. What can I do for you?"

He tipped his head towards me. "New."

She turned and smiled at me. "Hello. Welcome to the company. I'll get your paperwork printed in one minute. Shea, why don't you two have a seat?" She tilted her head towards two chairs in her cubicle and then spun back to type quickly on her computer.

I sat, but Shea remained standing.

"Do you know what position you're starting at today?" she asked me.

"No, ma'am," I answered immediately.

"No problem. Once you've got this filled out, bring them back to me," she informed me, stood, and pulled a stack of papers out of her printer. She put the papers in a manila folder and handed it to me. "Welcome."

I clutched the papers to my chest and stood.

Shea turned and headed back towards the elevators.

I walked quickly to catch up to his long strides and slid into the elevator.

"Breathe," he ordered me.

I took a breath.

The doors opened and I stared at the hallway before us that seemed to stretch on forever.

"This is the executive floor," Shea said.

As we walked down the hallway, we passed ten doors, each one with a name placard that blended in with the door.

At the end of the hallway there was a left turn that was completely unnoticeable from the other end. We turned, and there were two large double doors with closed blinds. Just outside the doors were two desks, where Forrest and Dane both sat.

They looked up as we approached and smiled.

Dane wore black slacks and a black shirt that made him almost blend in with his black chair.

Forrest, on the other hand, had on tan slacks and a dark green shirt that made him stand out from the mostly white office and his black chair.

"Hello, beautiful," Dane said, stood, and came to kiss my cheek.

Forrest gave me an appraising look and nodded. "That's a great outfit."

The black slacks and teal blouse were ones that I'd chosen first at the very first store we had been to the day before.

"Thank you," I replied.

"He's just finishing up a meeting," Dane told me. "Once that meeting is over, you'll be able to go in and talk to him."

I nodded and adjusted my grip on the packet of papers I carried.

"You can set those down on my desk, if you want," Forrest offered.

I took him up on the offer, set them down, and then leaned my hip on his desk. "So, this is where you two work?"

"Yep," he replied.

I scowled at his mostly empty desk. "No tea?"

He stuck his bottom lip out in a pout that I instantly wanted to grab with my teeth. "My favorite barista doesn't work at the local coffee shop anymore."

I rolled my eyes. "My employees can make the same cup of tea."

He shook his head. "No, they never put the right amount of milk in."

The urge to lean over his desk and kiss him was hard, but I straightened and said, "Well, maybe your girlfriend will make you some in the mornings."

His eyes brightened and he leaned forward to ask, "Girlfriend, huh? That's rather presumptuous of you."

Brushing down my shirt and pants, I said, "Says the man who bet to have me work in the same building as you and then insisted I move in. Then, pouted until I took the bedroom right next to his."

He beamed with smugness written all over his handsome face. "Damn straight I did."

The double doors opened and two angry men in suits with long, tied back hair and similar faces stormed out. They gave us a glare, hardly giving me a glance, and hurried around the corner.

Stephan stepped out, wiping his hands off with a towel, saw me, and smiled. "Good morning, Amelia. I hope your morning is going well so far?"

I nodded. "Yes, thank you."

"Come on in to my office. Bring your packet of papers, please," he said. He looked at Shea and said, "Ensure those two leave peacefully."

Shea nodded and left.

The packet felt even heavier when I picked it up again and followed Stephan into his office.

This room was incredibly ostentatious and felt nothing like him. It reminded me of the movies when they showed an evil billionaire's office. The floor was the same as the rest of the building, but there were some geometric patterned rugs near the back, where a full bar, a couch, and a few leather chairs sat.

Did he hold meetings there?

The desk was frosted glass with a laptop, keyboard, mouse, and one fountain pen. The chair behind it looked like it was white leather.

I made a note never to enter this room when it was that time of the month for me. No chances should be had.

"What's with the scowl?" Stephan asked and shut the office door.

"This office doesn't feel like you," I finally admitted.

He shrugged. "It's the type of persona they expect from a CEO like me."

Instead of going to the desk, he led me to the drinking area and waved at the leather chairs.

"These are more comfortable." He sat on the couch and draped his arms across the back. "So, do you know what position you want?"

I shook my head.

"Well, for now, let's get your background paperwork going," he said.

I set my driver's license on the table, opened the manila folder, and pulled out the stack.

He shuffled through the papers, pulled out two forms, and set them in front of me. "Fill these out."

"You know you don't have to do this, right? You could have just let me deal with HR," I said as I filled it out.

"I don't want them to know I'm allowing you to pick your position," he admitted.

"This building is gorgeous." I spoke so there weren't any awkward silences while I tried to remember all the important numbers and dates.

"Thank you. It took me six months to decide on the interior design alone," he said.

I finished the forms and slid them towards him.

He set his fingertips on the papers and met my gaze. "Anything else you need to tell me before this is run?"

I swallowed. "No other major issues."

His left brow rose. "Amelia—"

"How thorough is this background check?" I asked.

His lip twitched. "Very."

With a sigh, I leaned back in the chair, and tilted my head back to look up at the ceiling. "I've worked several types of jobs in several cities. That's really all I need to say about that."

"Hm." Stephan stood. "You and I will talk later. Secrets are not allowed in our family."

I dropped my chin and said, "But you're holding back my

secret from them."

He sighed dramatically. "Yes, because it is my belief that everyone has a right to tell their story when they are ready. Had you not started work so soon with me, I would not have pried about your past."

"Well, I'm not ready to talk about the other stuff," I said. "Besides, there's not much to tell. It just sucked."

He opened the door and stuck the papers and my ID out the door. "Get this to HR for processing, please. You are not to view the results until after I do."

"What?" Dane asked from outside.

"I'm serious, Dane. I want to read the results of the background check first. No one else is allowed to discuss or read it. You understand?"

"Yeah, sure," Dane said. "I hear you, boss. Just not sure why you're being all cryptic and weird about Amelia."

Stephan shut the door and returned to the couch. "Now, I want you to tell me what types of jobs you do enjoy. Or ones that you would want to do."

"Being your driver doesn't sound too bad, and since I'm living with you now, it would be pretty simple. What would I do during the day, like now, when you don't need a driver, though?"

"I could put you in the mailroom. They already have enough staff, so you coming and going won't affect them." He tapped his chin thoughtfully, then suddenly snapped his fingers. "I've got it!" Without any warning, he jumped up and walked out of the office.

I stared after him, wondering if I was supposed to follow.

Dane walked in and asked, "Where did he go?"

I shrugged. "He said he figured out what job I was going to do and then just left."

Dane sat in the other leather chair and set his hands in his lap. "So, want to tell me something?"

"What?" I asked.

His eyes looked like they sparkled in this bright room. "Why is Stephan being so secretive about your background check?"

Crap.

"I, uh...you see—"

"Dane, I've found the perfect job for Amelia," Stephan said, coming back into the room and saving me from answering Dane.

"What is that?" Dane asked and gave me a frown that told me he wasn't going to let this go.

"She's going to be my driver and my filer," Stephan said with a huge smile.

I looked around the office, but there weren't any filing cabinets. "Filer of what?" I asked.

Dane chuckled. "We have an entire room of filing cabinets and at least one cabinet full of papers that need to be filed."

My eyes widened and I smiled. "Oh, I love filing. I can be your filer. But what about once I get caught up on your backlog?"

"Oh, the paperwork is neverending," Dane said.

"I'm surprised a technology company doesn't keep everything digitally," I said.

Stephan shrugged. "I like having hardcopy backups to my important documents."

"The room has one of the most advanced fire systems in it," Dane said. "If you even flick a lighter, it activates."

"Is it one of the ones that sucks the air out?" I asked nervously.

Dane and Stephan nodded.

Stephan noticed my discomfort and said, "It has a protocol to wait to engage until after humans are out."

"How does it know if humans are out?" I asked. I'd watched a movie once where the security system had killed a ton of employees to try to keep a virus from spreading. I did not want to be killed because someone lit a match.

"It has heartbeat sensors," he said with a wide smile.

What? I'd never heard of such advanced technology before.

"If you'd prefer," Stephan said, "we could have the documents that need to be sorted moved to an office for you to work in. Then, when you're ready to file them, Dane or Forrest can assist you and ensure no fires are started and you're safe."

"I can even bring in masks and an oxygen tank if it will make you feel better," Dane offered.

"I would prefer to have an office to sort them in first," I said. "I need a lot of space to spread things out. First, I need to look at your filing to figure out your organization structure." My brain whirled quickly as I began thinking of how I was going to sort the papers and then create beautifully organized stacks.

"Wonderful!" Stephan said with a smile. "Now, let's talk wages." He walked to his desk, picked up his pen, and grabbed a notepad I hadn't seen on the desk. He jotted down something, walked to me, and held it out.

I looked down at the number on the paper. "Yearly?" I asked.

He threw his head back and laughed. "You're hilarious." When I didn't laugh or agree I was being funny, his smile wilted. "Amelia, that is your monthly salary."

I looked down at the number, at Stephan, at the number, at Dane, and back at the number. "No."

Dane peeked over my shoulder and asked, "You want more?"

I gasped and took a step to the side so I could look at them both. "Are you insane? This is a ridiculous sum. My business doesn't even make this amount."

Stephan and Dane scowled.

"I thought you said business was picking up?" Dane asked.

I bit my lower lip. Dammit, I hadn't meant to admit that.

"That's beside the point," I countered.

"That is an appropriate amount because you are a confidential employee dealing with documents that are not seen by anyone aside from the signing parties, usually. So, we are paying you to ensure you keep things secret and don't divulge them to the outside," Stephan explained.

I looked back at the number on the notepad. "You're going to find a way to pay me this much no matter what I say, aren't you?"

Dane laughed. "She knows you so well already, boss. Quick learner."

"Let's finish filling out your paperwork so we can turn it into HR," Stephan said and sat back down on the couch.

Dane continued to scowl at me as I walked over and took my seat again.

An hour later, I had filled out all of the forms, got my direct deposit set up, my badge, and was on my way to see my new office.

Forrest walked beside me silently, staring straight ahead as we made our way down the hallway.

"Are you giving me the silent treatment for a reason?" I asked with a wide smile.

He looked down at me, looked over at a door to our left, and said, "This office is available."

The door was unlocked, so I walked in and looked around. It was huge! There was a desk, couch, and a conference table. The conference table would be perfect for organizing the papers.

"This office will be perfect," I said and spun around with a wide smile.

Forrest closed the door behind him and leaned against it. "We need to talk."

My heart hammered in my chest and I took a few steps back. The comments of the sales clerks replayed in my head and I wished I'd brought something with me, even a pen.

"Wh-what are we going to talk about?" I asked.

He scowled and straightened. "Amelia, I'm not going to hurt you."

"Then why did you lead me to a secluded part of the floor, to an abandoned office, and why is the door closed?" I asked.

Our gazes locked and he looked hurt.

With slow movements, he grabbed a chair from the conference table and sat in it. "Does this make you feel safer?"

Seeing as how he could jump up and crack my neck in one movement...not really.

"Yes," I lied.

"You've been acting weird ever since we went to the mall. Dane mentioned it to me, too. Also, why is Stephan treating your background check so secretively? What is it that you aren't telling us?" He asked it all in a soft voice, no anger, just curiosity and what seemed like sadness.

Treating them differently because of rumors wasn't fair. They'd been nothing but kind to me, and had gone above and beyond to keep me safe many times. Yet, I felt like there was something they were hiding as well.

"What aren't you all telling me? There's no way that you four haven't found girlfriends who could handle your weird schedules and living arrangement by now. You guys latched on to me pretty fast and tight once you realized I wasn't scared of a polyamorous relationship. And I've been hearing a lot of rumors about you guys that has me wondering what is really going on with your quartet."

His eyebrows rose above eyes that had gone wide. "Rumors? Like what?"

That was the part he focused on?

"My past is...complicated. I don't like talking about it. If I talk about it, I might end up crying, or you might end up running away from me. I don't want that. I told Stephan because he was going to find out about it on the background report. I told him so that he wouldn't be blindsided today. We're all still getting to know each other and I didn't want to ruin it by talking about something I did in the past. I'm not that person anymore and I don't ever want to be her again." Even though I hadn't mentioned specifics, the fear and anxiety rose and tears welled in my eyes. I tilted my head back and looked up at the overhead lights to try to stop my tears.

"Babe, I swear I won't let anything happen to you while I'm with you. You're safe with me. You're safe with the others, too. We'd all put ourselves in front of a bullet for you," he said softly.

"Can...can we talk about this later? If I cry now, I won't be able to fix my makeup and I don't think Stephan wants me walking around with mascara down my face." I sniffled and took a few deep breaths to calm down.

"We can finish this discussion later as long as you promise to tell me what rumors you heard. I can't tell you if they're true or not if you don't tell me what they are," he said.

No longer on the verge of crying, I dropped my head and looked at him. He was still in the chair, but leaned forward, like he wanted to get up and come to me. I walked over and sat sideways on his lap and kissed his lips lightly, so I wouldn't get lipstick on him. "I'm sorry."

He brushed my hair back from my face and kissed my cheek. "I'm sorry I frightened you. I don't want you to ever be afraid of me."

His cologne was barely detectable until you got right up to his neck. I inhaled and brushed my nose against his neck. "You smell really good."

He arched his neck a bit and then leaned back. "No teasing,

okay?"

"Sorry." I bit my lip.

I started to stand up, but he grabbed my hips and held me in place. He moved one hand up my side, brushing the side of my breast and making me gasp softly. He continued brushing his hand up and then flicked my hair away from my neck. Slowly, he leaned forward and pressed a gentle kiss to my neck.

My body arched into his automatically and a soft moan slipped past my lips.

Sitting on his lap, I felt his instant reaction to the movement and the sound I made. His grip on my hip tightened and he nipped my neck.

"What are the rules about interoffice affairs?" I breathed.

Forrest groaned. "You are an evil little, sexy temptress. Trust me, I want to continue this, but our first time is not going to be on a conference table."

My lower body tensed as I imagined being bent over the table with Forrest behind me.

"You sure?" I asked.

He stood and set me on my feet. "Honey, we've got to get back to Stephan's office. We don't have enough time for the things I plan to do to you."

"Now who's a tease?" I asked, and pouted.

He adjusted his pants and cleared his throat. "Come on, let's tell Stephan you've chosen your office."

I followed behind him, smiling at the fact that I had such an effect on the big man. Oh, we were going to use that conference table. Maybe not today, but definitely soon.

"Stop staring at my ass and get your mind out of the gutter," he ordered me without turning around.

He did have a nice ass. "I can look all I want," I countered.

Dane looked up from the desk at Forrest, glanced at me, then looked back at Forrest.

"Go on in and tell Stephan you picked office two," Forrest told me as he walked to stand in front of Dane's desk.

"Okay," I said softly and hurried into the ostentatious office once more.

Stephan looked up from a pile of papers he was reading at his desk and asked, "You picked one already?"

I nodded. "Forrest called it office two."

Stephan smiled. "That's a perfect office. It's just around the corner, so you won't be far from us or the filing room." He thumped the stack of papers on his desk. "I got your background check back."

My heart fell. That huge stack was my background check?

"I think it's time we brought the boys in and you told them everything," he said with a gentle smile.

"I don't have makeup with me," I whispered.

"You want to make them wait until tonight?" he asked. "That's a bit cruel."

"What are you going to do if they decide they don't want to continue dating me?" I asked and folded my arms across my chest. "You made me sign a twelve-month deal to work just around the corner from them."

"I did not *make* you do anything, Amelia," he said, and chuckled. "Trust me, they aren't going to react the way you think they are." Something on his phone chimed and he scowled as he looked at it. "Well, looks like your wish to postpone just got granted."

Lucky!

"Come on, you've got to drive me, though," he said as he stood.

"My first assignment," I said with a wide smile. "Where are we going?"

"A warehouse I own near the docks," he replied with a scary scowl. "I've got some business to finish there."

Chapter Twelve

We walked out and Stephan waved at Dane and Forrest, who were sitting close together, whispering about something.

Dane and Forrest stood, grabbed their jackets, and followed us to the elevator.

Inside the elevator, I stayed near the back, letting the three larger men block the way.

Stephan typed something on his phone and then looked at Forrest and said, "Shea and Arcadio are coming, too."

I scowled. "Do you need me to drive then?" If there were five of them, wouldn't I just be in the way?

"Yes," all three said at the same time.

Okay, then.

The doors opened to a parking garage and I followed them to a black SUV with windows tinted far darker than legal.

Dane handed me the keys and whispered, "Whatever you do, Babe, don't put yourself at risk for us, okay?"

I frowned. "What?"

"Promise me that if something happens, if the people we are talking to get out of hand, you'll leave us and go protect yourself?"

"If I'm a driver, my job is to take Stephan to and from his place. I'm not going to leave you guys stranded at some warehouse because I got scared," I said with narrowed eyes. "I'm not a baby or a chicken. I can handle some tense negotiations."

He sighed and pulled me into a hug. "Tonight, we all need to talk and be honest with each other. Okay?"

"Sure," I whispered back.

He kissed the top of my head and climbed into the car.

Arcadio and Shea walked out of the elevator and climbed into the car, too.

I climbed in and chuckled at how far back the seat was from the pedals. Forrest or Shea must have driven last.

The guys buckled in while I pushed the button and waited for the electric seat to move forward enough for me to reach the pedals.

Time dragged on as the seat slid forward, whirring and moving me at what felt like centimeters by the minute.

Looks were exchanged as I waited for the seat to reach its proper spot, then I adjusted the back of the seat, the mirrors, and finally buckled myself in.

Stephan was smirking and turned away from me before asking, "Are you ready, Amelia?"

"Yes," I said, and started the SUV.

It roared to life and I backed out of the parking spot and headed out of the parking garage.

"Directions?" I asked.

Stephan input the address into the SUV's navigation system and sat back again. "Amelia, you are to remain in the car. Do not come in for any reason. Arcadio, you stay with Amelia. The rest of you will come with me."

"You sure, boss?" Arcadio asked.

Stephan turned to glance at him with a severe scowl. "Don't question me again, Arcadio."

Arcadio bobbed his head. "Yes, boss."

This was a completely different dynamic than the one they had at home. Everyone looked tense and the atmosphere was thick with testosterone and aggression.

What was going on?

I followed the directions the navigation system gave me and parked on the side of a large warehouse right next to the docks. The sound of crashing waves and seagulls were the only things I could hear.

Ahead of us sat a black SUV, very similar to ours, with a muscular man in a suit with sunglasses on in the driver's seat.

"Do whatever Arcadio tells you to," Stephan ordered me. "Do you understand, Amelia?"

I nodded my head. "Yes."

He nodded and climbed out of the SUV.

Dane, Shea, and Forrest kissed my cheek before they climbed out after Stephan, all with their suit jackets on and stern expressions on their faces.

Arcadio cocked a gun behind me, making me wince. "Don't worry, Amelia, I'll protect you."

I looked over at the driver of the other car and saw him set a handgun on the dashboard of his car. What the hell were they involved in?

"Do you have a spare gun?" I asked Arcadio.

"What?" he asked.

"Arcadio, I can shoot. If these guys are going to fire at us, I'd feel a lot better if I had a gun I could use, too," I told him. I did not want to shoot someone, but if it was my life or theirs, I would not hesitate.

"Center console," he told me.

I opened it and my mouth dropped. Four handguns and about a dozen magazines were strapped into the side of the console, which was much larger inside then it looked on the outside.

"What type of Tardis sorcery is this?" I whispered, grabbed a handgun and a magazine, and set them on the passenger seat.

"You're a geek?" Arcadio asked.

I turned to look at him and asked, "The fantasy books on my bookshelf didn't give that away?"

He chuckled. "I guess I just didn't think about it."

"Well, I'm not ashamed of my nerdiness or my love of raunchy fantasy books," I told him. "And if you're going to date me, you're going to have to accept that side of me."

He leaned forward and whispered in my ear, "Why don't you find one of those passages in your raunchy fantasy books and I'll make it reality?"

Holy orcs, I'd thought my panties were soaked earlier from Forrest, but now I wondered if I was getting the car's seat wet.

"Aren't we supposed to be watching out for trouble?" I asked, my voice rough. "You're distracting me."

"Promises for the future, gorgeous," he whispered, but went back to surveying our surroundings for threats.

"Why are we worried something crazy is going to happen?" I asked.

"These business partners have been difficult to deal with. They insist on meeting in shady areas and then try to force Stephan into shitty deals. He's decided he has had enough and is going to stand his ground today. We just want to be alert in case they decide to get aggressive," he explained.

"And by aggressive, you mean shooting at us?" I asked.

"Yeah," he answered nonchalantly.

Right. Getting shot at was totally nothing. Totally normal when doing deals with business partners.

"Did you pick an office?" he asked.

I nodded. "Yep. I've got a big desk, a couch, and a conference table."

"Well, then that means there are at least three places we can enact one of your book fantasies on," he said.

Hell below...

"Forrest claimed first rights," I said, though that wasn't completely true.

Arcadio cursed beneath his breath. "Totally unfair."

The door to the warehouse opened just as gunshots sounded. Forrest, Shea, Stephan, and Dane ran out the door towards us.

I set the gun down, started the car, and backed up around the corner of the warehouse so they didn't have to run as far. Forrest and Dane stopped, turned around, and shot at the door just as someone tried to follow them.

Stephan jumped into the car as did Shea.

"I take it negotiations did not go well?" I asked, surprised at how calm I sounded.

"No," Stephan panted. "They did not."

Ahead of us, the driver we had been facing before grabbed the gun from the dashboard and leaned out the window of his door.

I rolled my window down, leaned out, and shot him in the shoulder twice. My third shot went wide and missed him completely.

He yelled in pain and slid back into his car.

"Go!" Forrest bellowed as he and Dane jumped into the car.

I handed Stephan the gun, butt first, and stomped on the gas pedal.

"Can we talk about Amelia being a badass just now?" Arcadio asked.

Another SUV swung around in the corner right in front of us, blocking our escape.

I slammed on my brakes, swung the car so the driver's side faced them, snatched the gun from Stephan, and shot at their windows and doors.

Arcadio opened his window and shot at them, too.

The driver backed up, deciding they didn't want to risk it, apparently.

I spun the wheel, stomped on the gas, and handed the gun to Stephan. "Reload, please."

"What is going on?" Dane asked. "Who are you?"

Stephan reloaded the gun and held it out.

I grabbed it. As soon as we passed the parked SUV, I opened fire so they wouldn't try to shoot us while we passed. Finally out of the warehouse area and to a road, I handed the gun back, spun the wheel and floored it onto the road.

"Directions," I snapped.

"Left, right, left, left," Stephan replied, but began typing in an address into the navigation system as well.

I followed his directions, which lead us to downtown. "Downtown?" I asked.

"They won't shoot at us here," Stephan said and relaxed in his seat.

We merged into traffic, inching forward slower than a turtle.

"Stephan!" Shea snapped. "What aren't you telling us about her? What isn't she telling us about herself?"

Something hit Shea's window, making him jump.

We all turned and saw one of the SUVs with their guys shooting at us from the alley, where others couldn't see us.

"Bulletproof glass?" I asked.

Stephan nodded. "All of our cars have it."

"They're likely to miss us and hit pedestrians," I said. How could I get them to stop shooting at us while not putting us in danger?

"We will discuss Amelia later," Stephan said. "Let's get to safety first."

Just ahead was a parking structure. If we could get them to follow us, we could take them up to the top to fewer pedestrians.

"I have a plan, but it'll require us to have a shootout," I said.

Stephan arched a brow. "We generally try to avoid shootouts."

"Okay, well we either sit here and get shot at, or we take them to a safer place and fight them head on," I said and shrugged.

"Who are you and what have you done with Amelia?" Forrest asked.

I looked around and realized the park to our left was empty, and on the opposite side of the park traffic was moving freely towards the freeway. Luck was definitely on our side since the park was normally full of people. What time was it? Maybe it was because everyone was working or in school.

"Buckle up," I ordered them. "Please make sure the safety is on your guns."

Stephan checked the safety, put it in the console, and everyone put their belts on.

I double checked there were no pedestrians and made a totally illegal left turn, driving across the grass, through the park.

"See, I knew you'd make a great driver," Stephan said and beamed as we bounced through and into traffic.

The person I cut off honked their horn angrily.

Raising my hand, I waved in an apology, then hurried the final block before we merged onto the freeway.

"So, where are we going?" I asked.

"Back to the office," Stephan said. "We have more work to do."

"It's actually lunch time," Shea said.

"We can order in," Stephan offered.

"I vote we go home and talk about the elephant in the shape of a sweet woman in the room," Forrest said.

I hadn't meant to revert to my past self and give away some of things I was capable of. I'd come to this city to start over, and now I might have ruined it all.

Stephan let out a long sigh. "Fine. I can see you won't do any work today. Amelia, please drive us home."

"Can you put the address in, please? I don't have it memorized," I said.

The drive to the house was completely silent and I could feel four sets of eyes boring a hole in the back of my head.

I parked and ran inside and to my room to get changed first, before they could ask me anything. Once changed into sweatpants and a baggy t-shirt I'd stolen from Dane, I stared at my reflection and swallowed hard. My heart pounded in my chest and my hands shook slightly as I prepared to go back out there and tell them about my past.

With a glare at myself to saddle up, I walked back out to the living room where the five men waited.

Shea, Forrest, Dane, and Arcadio all sat on the couch, most with unreadable expressions on their faces. This might be the last time I talked to them. This might be the end of our relationships.

"Amelia, you only need to tell us what you're comfortable telling us," Stephan said. He sat on a chair he'd grabbed from the dining room instead of opting to join the other four on the couch. Not that there would have been room with both Shea and Forrest there.

"No, bullshit. She needs to be honest with us," Dane snapped.

I flinched and sat on the ground on the other side of the coffee table, so it was between me and them on the couch. "I should have told you sooner, but I didn't have any intention of moving in with you this soon. So, I'd like to point out that you forced me to move in here. I wanted you to get to know me better before I told you about my past. Arcadio and Shea haven't even gone on a date with me yet."

"We've been talking to you for months," Arcadio countered. "We've been building up our friendship with you."

He was right, but it wasn't the same.

"Okay, but you have to tell me what's really going on with you guys. I guarantee the CEO of Bapple isn't dealing with shootouts and shady deals by the docks." No one argued with that. "Do you want the long version or short version?" I asked.

"Long," they all said simultaneously.

"Then I'm going to need water and tissues before we start," I said, and stood.

Only three steps later, the window to my right exploded, glass shards pelted me, most getting stuck in my clothes and hair, but many in my skin.

My ears rang and I stumbled forward, my vision blurred so that I couldn't tell where the wall or the floor was as it swayed around in front of me.

Someone grabbed me around the waist and picked me up. They carried me outside and I really hoped it was Shea or Forrest.

The person carrying me tossed me into an SUV, while gunshots rang out around me.

I cried out in pain as their toss made me land on areas of my skin that had glass in it.

So, it definitely had not Shea or Forrest who grabbed me then.

My vision became a little more stable, so I could finally see what was going on. The person who tossed me in the car faced away from me, blocking the door, while shooting towards the house. The driver stood and shot over the top of the car, and there were two more guys around the back of the car.

No one was paying attention to me.

The man who blocked my door was tall, so tall that the back of his knees were close to the open door. I had to time this right, or I could put the guys in more danger.

Squatted down, I kicked the back of the guy's right knee, making it fold and making his body drop slightly. Before he could react, I wrapped my arms around his throat and put him in a chokehold. He batted at my arm and tried to punch me, but couldn't. He grabbed for my hair, but thankfully I had put it in a ponytail.

He stumbled away from the SUV and his buddies stopped shooting.

I swung my leg around and slammed my heel into his crotch as hard as I could. He gasped and fell to his knees.

His buddies aimed their guns at me, but couldn't get a clear shot because I hid behind his giant head.

"Back off," I warned them. Slowly, I backed up, but the guy I had wouldn't budge. He was too damned heavy.

On his left side he had a holster with a handgun. Why he didn't have his jacket on over it, I wasn't sure, but it was perfect for me. I grabbed the gun and slammed the butt into his head to ensure he was knocked out and wouldn't attack me. I aimed the gun at the driver's body through the open window.

"You have ten seconds to get in the car and drive out of here or I'm going to blow your friend's brains out," I threatened.

"Little lady, you don't know what you're doing," one of the men said.

I aimed the gun at one of the back windows, near where they were hiding and squeezed the trigger. The glass exploded and they all ducked. "Nine! Eight!" I yelled.

"This isn't over," one of them said as they climbed in the car.

They all looked at their unconscious friend in front of me, but seemed to decide he was a lost cause.

I aimed the gun at his head, just to hammer home my threat.

They backed out of the driveway and down the road.

As soon as they were gone, I dropped the guy, put the safety on the gun, and slumped to the ground, crying.

"Babe?" Dane asked softly.

"I've got cuts and glass all over," I cried. "It hurts."

"Can you walk? I don't want to pick you up and hurt you more," Dane said.

I stood, and Dane held my hand as we walked. "I thought it was Forrest or Shea who grabbed me," I said while crying, sobs breaking up my words. "I didn't know until he tossed me it wasn't them. Because they would never toss me like that when I was hurt."

"No, we wouldn't," Shea said.

"Get the kit," Dane said. "We're going to have to pick the glass out of her."

"I'm sorry," I cried. "I'm sorry I didn't tell you about my past. I'm sorry they tried to kidnap me."

"Shh," Dane said gently. "We'll talk about everything after we get you patched up."

"Is anyone hurt?" I asked.

"No, we're all fine. You're the most injured," Shea said behind us.

"I hate crying," I said, and cried harder.

"It'll be alright," Dane whispered and squeezed my hand. "We'll get you all fixed up and in comfy clothes with a cup of hot cocoa."

"With mint?" I asked, and sniffled.

"With mint," he said, and smiled down at me.

Chapter Thirteen

Cup of cocoa in hand, bandages on a lot of my body, I sat before them once again. Water and tissues sat on the table before me, just in case.

"My mom was in a polyamorous relationship with my dad and two other boyfriends. I was raised by them all. There was a man in town who was obsessed with my mom, but he was a creep, so she didn't give him the time of day. One weekend when all of her guys were out of town camping, the creep came. I threatened him with one of our guns, but he was belligerent. He pulled a gun out and I shot him before he could shoot my mom, and he died. I lived in a small town, and unfortunately one of the deputies was related to the creep. So, they took me in and arrested me. It was later determined it was self-defense, but it's still on my record. After that, I left our little town and went to one of the largest cities I could find. Since I had a record, I didn't try to get good jobs. I took crappy jobs that mostly paid under the table, some that had me running for my life.

"I started dating this guy I met at work and it wasn't until I caught him passed out on the couch with the needle still in his arm that I found out he was a druggie. The signs were all there, but I was young and naïve. I left, but he begged his dealer to send some of his guys after me. Three of them found me, chained me up, and kept me in a basement for a week to teach me a lesson about trying to run from them. One of the men took pity on me, stole me, and hid me away. He taught me to fight and to shoot. The dealer found out somehow that I was living with him and told him it was me or his job. Before they could kill me, I escaped. I roamed from town to town, living in my car and saving my money to open up a café of my own. While I roamed, I kept up my shooting practice at random indoor gun ranges, renting their guns since I didn't own any myself. I also took lessons at some of the martial arts places just to keep my skills fresh in case my past came back. The café is mine, but it's not doing well and honestly, I'm probably going to have to close it soon. I'm sorry I didn't tell you all this, but...it's embarrassing. I don't like knowing how to do the things I know. I don't like shooting people or hurting them. They're skills I picked up out of necessity. I came here for a new start, to be a new person, the person I wanted to be when I was younger."

All five men stared in silence.

I sipped my mint cocoa and hummed at its deliciousness. So good.

"Is that all?" Forrest asked.

I thought about it a moment. "Unless you want me to detail how many men I've slept with, yes."

"We'll pass on that," Dane said quickly.

"Now, it's your turn," I said. "Who the hell are you people?" I glanced at the boarded-up window and wondered what they'd done with the man I'd knocked out.

"In addition to being a CEO of a technology company, I'm also the boss of the largest mob in the surrounding five states," Stephan said.

"Mob?" I asked.

He nodded.

"What's your product?" I asked.

"Actually, we don't focus on selling products. I created a sex worker union. We have a house, well houses, since we have now opened five, that the women run their trade out of. Only women who are eighteen or older, completely willing, and clean – testing is done every month – can work for us. They get protection from our security, housing, health insurance, and even retirement accounts," he explained.

My mouth dropped.

"We do have a few subdivisions that sell drugs, but we limit their sales so we don't become a target for the FBI," Stephan added. "And they only focus on selling marijuana. Risking our exposure by selling hard drugs isn't worth it. Plus, I don't really want to fight the other mobs for territory on drugs."

The mob? They were in the mob.

I...I was in the...

"So, since I joined your company, am your driver, and am dating them, I'm also part of your mob?" I asked.

They all smiled.

"Yes," Stephan said. "I told you, you were part of our family."

Only I could become a mobster by accident.

I closed my eyes and let out a breath. Okay, this was fine. Everything was fine. My boss, and the men I was dating, were mobsters. But not really bad mobsters because they weren't selling women or anything.

"That's why the clerks said you were dangerous," I whispered.

"What?" Dane asked.

"The clerks at the clothing store were whispering about you guys being dangerous and thought I was in danger from you," I said.

Forrest's eyes widened. "That's why you've been acting weird. And why you were scared of me today."

I looked down at my cup and shrugged. "Maybe." After a moment I asked, "Are you going to tell me why your quartet really doesn't have a girlfriend by now?"

Dane chuckled. "You think any girl would be willing to handle getting shot at and having people attempt to kidnap her? That we could find someone able to mesh with all of us, including Stephan, who wasn't either mousy or power hungry? You are the first woman we've found that we all love spending time with and isn't just using us for our connections. You are the first woman who has been willing to accept our crazy work schedules and lives. You are the only woman that fits in during game nights and doesn't pout or beg for attention if the others are playing games."

Well, now that I knew they were mobsters, it did make a bit more sense why women wouldn't stick around. Was I stupid for staying? For possibly endangering myself?

"Are you five good?" Stephan asked.

Without moving my head, I raised my eyes so I could look at the guys beneath my lashes.

"I'm good," Forrest said with a smile.

"Me, too," Arcadio said.

"Yeah," Shea said.

"Are we?" Dane asked me.

"Well, I've never been part of a mob before, but I think it's a little late to back out now. Besides, I really like you guys," I said.

Dane leaned forward. "Are you saying you want to join our family? That you want to stay living here?"

"I'm saying that I don't want to leave and am willing to give it a shot," I said.

"Would you like to work on your room this weekend?" Stephan asked.

I shrugged. "Sure."

"Well, I'm going to leave you all to discuss your relationship things. I'm sorry you were hurt in my house. We will ensure it doesn't happen again," Stephan said.

"What did you do with the guy I knocked out?" I asked.

"One of our guys picked him up. They'll interrogate him and deal with him," Shea answered.

I blinked. "So, you guys don't interrogate or kill them?"

Stephan's smile was the widest I had ever seen it. "You're the only one in this room who has ever killed someone."

"What?" I screeched.

"Wow," Arcadio said, and chuckled. "I hadn't thought about that. You are the most badass out of all of us."

"I should probably be upset or intimidated by that," Forrest said. "Yet all I feel is turned on."

"We should take her to the range and see who the best shot is," Dane said.

I smirked. "You all better prepare your bets ahead of time."

Dane walked around to me, helped me stand, and hugged me, gently so he wouldn't hurt all the cuts on my body. "I'm sorry I didn't protect you."

Arcadio walked behind me and hugged me, too. "I'm sorry, too."

Forrest and Shea wrapped their arms around all of us. "I'm sorry, too," they said simultaneously.

"It's not your fault those assholes threw a grenade through the window just as I walked by," I whispered as I basked in their warmth. This was what I had wanted my entire life. To be surrounded by people who cared about me.

"We'd like to talk to you about setting up a calendar so we can keep track of our dates and important events," Forrest said.

They all stepped back from me and moved so I could see them without turning my head.

"Like, link our calendars on our phones?" I asked.

Shea shook his head. "Dane never checks his phone calendar. We'd need a physical one."

"I can order one and put it on the wall in my bedroom," I said with a wide smile. Last year I had found a bunch of organizational items I wanted and added a list to my favorite shopping site. One of those items was a yearly calendar that was dry erase. The calendar would need to be color coded, which meant I was going to buy the large pack of dry erase markers.

"Sounds good," Dane said.

"So, do I get paid for a full day today, even though we didn't work the full day?" I asked.

Everyone laughed.

I didn't find it that funny. I was actually being serious.

"You don't have to worry about your pay, Amelia," Shea said.

Looking at the large man I asked, "Why are you so different with me than you are at work?"

He shrugged. "I don't like talking to people."

"You talk to me," I countered.

"You're not people," he said. "You're Kitten."

I rolled my eyes, but a smile slipped on my face no matter how hard I tried to keep it straight. "Right." My feet hurt and I shifted on them.

"Are you in pain?" Forrest asked.

"A little," I admitted.

"Why don't you lie down and we'll watch a movie?" Arcadio suggested.

"Okay," I agreed and threw myself onto the couch. "Ow!" How I had forgotten that I was cut up that quickly, I didn't know, but I had.

"Don't make me carry you everywhere," Shea threatened me.

"Actually, before we start the movie, can I talk to Dane?" I asked.

Dane tensed. "Sure."

He helped me stand and hovered over me as we went down the hallway and to my room.

I shut the door and said, "I really am sorry for keeping all of that a secret from you. Are we good?"

He sat on the edge of my bed and held his arms open. Without hesitation, I walked into his arms and sat on his lap. He kissed me gently and said, "I'm sorry I didn't tell you about being in the mob, either. We're good. Just promise me no more secrets, okay?"

I nodded and threw my body weight against his upper body so he fell backwards with me on top. Between peppering kisses over his face I said, "Promise. No. More. Secrets."

He chuckled and pulled me down to lay on top of him. "When they snatched you out of the house, I felt my heart plummet. I've never been so scared about someone else before. Not even the guys, and we're basically brothers."

"It wasn't a picnic for me either," I whispered. "I promised myself I'd never be a victim again. That I wouldn't let someone tie me up and..." My words trailed off as I sniffled and fresh tears came.

Dane shifted us so that he was spooning me and stroked my hair. "We won't let that happen, Babe. Even if they had taken you, we would have been right behind them. They never would have gotten you into another house."

"But you'd have to kill them to do that," I sniffled.

He turned my head so I had to look at him and gave me a hard glare. "I'll kill every man in this state to keep you safe. I mean it."

My mouth dropped open and I shouted, "Why would you want to fight your friends?"

Dane rolled his eyes. "That is not what I said."

As I expected, my door opened and Forrest stood with his arms folded. "What's this?"

"She's twisting my words—"

"Dane said he could kick your butt," I said.

Forrest scoffed. "In his dreams, maybe."

Dane glared at Forrest. "Really? You still think you're a better fighter than me?"

"I know I am," Forrest said with a smug smile.

"What's going on?" Arcadio asked behind Forrest.

"Forrest and Dane said they could kick your ass," I told him.

"What?" Arcadio asked. "Are you guys drunk or delusional?"

"Well, we all know who's got the largest—" Shea started to say from the hallway, but all of them yelled his name and he stopped talking. I wished I could see him to see his face, but he was hidden behind Forrest, who still blocked my doorway.

"That is not what I said," Dane groaned.

It never failed. Men were testosterone, dick measuring, I'm better than you, tough guys. If you could get them to argue over who was stronger, or really any measuring contest, they'd go on for hours.

"Arm wrestling contest, now!" Forrest snapped.

I hopped off the bed and clapped my hands with a high-pitched squeal. "I love arm wrestling contests!"

Simultaneously, all of their phones chimed.

My arms fell to my sides and I let out a groan. Who was ruining my fun?

"Meeting," Forrest said. "Let's go."

Dane hopped up and followed Forrest into the hallway.

I plopped down onto my bed and pouted. I would have to rile them up again later to get my arm wrestling watching.

Dane poked his head into my room and frowned. "What are you doing? Come on."

I pointed at myself. "Me? Go to the meeting?"

He nodded. "Come on, mobsterina."

Mobsterina? I kind of liked the sound of that. I could wear a tutu and twirl around while shooting guys in their shoulders.

Dane grabbed my hand and dragged me down the hallway, around three turns, and into a room I'd never seen that had dark lights, a huge conference table, and a single phone in the center.

Everyone else, including Stephan, was already seated.

"Sorry, I didn't realize I was invited," I apologized. There were a few seats open, but before I had a chance to decide where to sit, Dane pulled me to the far side and pulled the seat out so I would sit between him and Forrest.

Stephan smiled. "Welcome to your first mob meeting."

I returned his smile. "Thanks."

"We got word back from our interrogator," Stephan said.

"Wait? You guys really have a separate interrogator?" I asked.

"Interrogation is a skill," Shea said. "You can't just punch someone and demand information."

"I mean, you *could*," I countered.

Shea rolled his eyes.

"What did they find out?" Dane asked, clearly trying to get the meeting back on topic.

"It was the Holmes Family," Stephan said.

"Is there a Watson Family, too?" I asked, realizing the names were very similar to books I'd read.

Dane dropped his head with a sigh. "Babe, can you save questions for after Stephan tells us everything?"

I put a serious face on and looked at Stephan. "Right. Sorry. Please continue."

Stephan's lip twitched. "The Holmes Family found out

about Amelia, but we aren't sure how. Obviously, my mansion's location isn't secret, so they knew right where to find us."

"Are we moving to the other house?" Forrest asked.

Other house? They had another house?

Stephan nodded. "I don't like having to drive so far for work, but I'm not going to let them hurt one of my family again. Start packing. I'd like to leave no later than midnight."

My phone rang and I cringed. "Sorry. I should have put that on vibrate." I quickly left the room to answer. "Hello?"

"Amelia Howard?" a man asked.

"Who wants to know?" I asked back.

"This is Officer Smith with the Police Department. Your café is on fire and we'd like you to come down and answer a few questions," he said.

"My café is on fire?" I screamed. "Is the fire department there?"

"Yes, ma'am, they are currently working on putting it out," he said.

I burst back into the room and they all turned to me. "My café is on fire!"

They raced out of the room, sweeping me along as they ran to a side door that lead to a garage.

Chapter Fourteen

"We're on our way," I told the officer.

"We?" he asked, but I hung up instead of answering.

"My café is on fire," I repeated over and over as we climbed into the SUV. Arcadio drove, which was probably best.

"Kitten," Shea whispered beside me.

I looked up at him, tears in my eyes. "My café is on fire."

He pulled my seatbelt around and buckled it for me. "I know, Kitten. It's okay. We'll get there and we'll find out what happened."

It took us fifteen minutes to get to the café and tears slid down my cheeks when I saw the burned down building that used to be mine. Somehow, the building beside it remained intact. Probably due to the firemen's work.

"It's...gone," I whispered, my lower lip quivering.

An officer approached our vehicle and we all climbed out. Shea walked behind me while Dane and Forrest walked to each side.

Arcadio and Stephan walked ahead of us and intercepted the officer. The officer spoke to them and glanced at me every few seconds.

Stephan shook the officer's hand, turned, and came over to me. "No one was inside. It happened after it was closed. They know it was arson, but don't have a confirmation on a suspect yet."

"I never got an alarm installed," I said. "Because they wouldn't install at my building for some reason."

"They're not going to question you because I explained you were working or with us the whole time," Stephan added.

I looked at the table Dane and Forrest always used, but it was just a smoldering pile of ash now. Seeing it broke me and I fell to my knees and sobbed.

Years I had saved up. Years I had taken awful jobs and lived in terrible conditions just to open that place. I hadn't even been open a year yet and it was all gone.

Shea picked me up and cradled me against his chest. "I'm sorry, Kitten. We'll find out who did this and we'll make them pay. I promise."

I buried my head against his chest and bawled like a child who had lost their favorite toy.

The world blurred around me. Somehow, we returned to the house and I had no memory of how we got there except for Shea's arms around me, holding me. He held me while we drove, held me while he walked into the house, and held me on the couch where he sat and stroked my head.

"A decade wasted," I whispered, the tears finally cried out.

"It wasn't wasted," Shea argued. "You saved and completed a goal that most would never achieve. Yes, it's gone now, but you still did it."

"May I see your phone?" Stephan asked me.

I slid it out of my pocket and handed it to him without question.

"I know this isn't the best time, but we do need to pack so

that we can leave," Shea said. "Do you want to come to my room and stay with me while I pack?"

I nodded.

He stood and carried me to his room, setting me gently down on the bed, and then started tossing clothes and things into duffel bags.

Dane peeked in, but after seeing me on the bed, he left again.

"Oh, I completely forgot about this," Shea said.

I looked over at him and saw a black velvet bag in his hand.

He set it on the bed in front of me and smiled wide. "It's your gift. From the bet you won."

Since no more tears would come and the shock was almost gone, I sat up and opened the bag. Inside was a black box. Inside of the black box was a necklace with a diamond cat pendant.

One corner of my lip twitched and I looked up at Shea. "You got me a kitten necklace."

He knelt before me, took the necklace out, and put it on me. "Yes, I did."

I threw my arms around him and kissed his cheek. "Thank you."

"Oy, stop necking," Arcadio yelled. "More packing. Less necking."

"Necking?" Shea yelled back. "What are you, eighty?"

"Eighty inches!" Arcadio responded.

"You change into a truck all of a sudden?" Forrest asked from somewhere in the house.

"Why you have to chime in?" Arcadio grumbled.

With a chuckle, I stood and brushed myself off. "Okay, I'm going to go pack."

"You want me to come with you?" he asked. "I'm almost done."

"I'm okay," I said. "I can't change the past and since no one was hurt, I just need to get over the inanimate objects being destroyed. I've got a new job that pays a lot and in the future, if I wanted to, I can open a new café with the insurance money I received."

He smiled. "Right."

"Oh, I guess I need to call my employees," I said, and cringed.

"Already taken care of," Stephan said from the doorway. "And, I let them know they'll be getting a month's worth of wages so they can look for a job without worrying."

"Y-you took care of it?" I stammered.

He smiled and held out my phone. "Yes. I told you, Amelia, you are part of my family now, and I take care of my family."

I threw my arms around his neck and hugged him. "Thank you."

He squeezed me once and then released me. "Now, you need to hurry and pack. We've got to get to the other house."

I nodded and hurried down the hallway. "Yes, sir."

"Why can't you all be as cooperative as her?" Stephan asked.

It took me less than ten minutes to get all of the things I had packed into a suitcase. Forrest carried it out to the garage and I followed behind him, admiring the view.

"So, do I still get my own room at this new house?" I asked.

Forrest glanced over his shoulder at me and said, "Nope."

"What?" I asked, not having expected that answer.

"You're going to have to room hop between us all," he said and held open the garage door.

I stepped past him and frowned. "Oh."

"He's teasing you," Stephan said from beside the SUV. "I've got at least five rooms you can choose from."

"Come on, Stephan. Let me tease her a little bit before you

ruin my fun," Forrest complained and tossed my suitcase in the back with everyone else's.

"I could just let her share my bed," Stephan said and smiled brightly. "Her virtue would be safest with me."

I laughed and a snort came out. "Virtue."

"Did...did you just snort?" Forrest asked.

"No," I lied immediately.

"She totally snorted," Shea said from inside the SUV.

"Did not," I countered. "I'm a lady, and ladies do not snort."

"You are not a lady and you definitely snorted," Dane said.

"Well, I only snort when something is really funny," I replied, and climbed into the backseat to sit between Arcadio and Forrest. Dane was in the driver's seat and Stephan and Shea were in the middle seat.

Dane turned around to look at me, sticking his head between the two front seats. "Are you implying that I've not been funny enough to make you snort?" he asked.

I shrugged. "If the shoe fits..."

His mouth dropped. "Wow."

"Let's go," Stephan said.

Dane turned around and started the vehicle. "I've just been challenged, Stephan."

Stephan sighed. "You take everything as a challenge, Crackers."

"How did you choose all of their nicknames?" I asked.

Stephan turned sideways in his seat so he could look back at me without straining his neck. "Well, Dane loved crackers when we were younger. He was always crunching on them. We'd be in the middle of an assembly and he'd pull out a sleeve of crackers and offer them to us. I swore he had a box in his backpack and went through it each day. I don't know how his mother afforded his cracker addiction."

"I bought my own crackers," Dane replied. "I mowed the old people's lawns."

"To afford your cracker addiction?" I asked, trying not to laugh.

"Yes," he replied. We drove out of the garage and down the super private street lined with mansions.

"He still keeps a box of crackers in his room," Shea said.

"What are you doing going in my room?" Dane asked and glanced at Shea in the rearview mirror, scowling.

"I bet he's got at least two boxes in his luggage in the back," Forrest said.

"Leave my shit alone!" Dane growled.

Stephan's smile widened. "Shea's nickname should be obvious. He's always been one of the largest guys we've known. Since we didn't want to call him a pig or something else rude, I chose ox. They're hard workers and so is Shea."

"Hard headed, too," I added.

Stephan laughed. "Yes. Yes he is."

"What about Forrest?" I asked. His was the one I was most curious about.

"Flowers here was notorious for falling out of the windows of girls' bedrooms and into rosebushes. I can't tell you the number of times I had to pick thorns out of his ass," Stephan explained. "It got to the point that we kept a pair of tweezers and bandages under the coffee table."

"Why didn't you call him thorns or scratches then?" I asked.

Stephan shook his head. "We were fifteen. I wasn't going to give him a cool name for being an idiot. No, he got flowers for constantly falling into the flowers when fleeing a girl's dad, or later on their husband or boyfriend."

"You're a homewrecker?" I asked and looked at Forrest.

He shrugged. "I didn't force them. If I hadn't been there,

some other guy would have. I stopped that once we graduated anyway."

"Okay, what about Arcadio?" I asked.

"Well, once you see him in hand to hand combat, it will make a bit more sense. He's fast and vicious and it reminded me of a jackal," Stephan explained. "He wanted to be called a wolf or something else, but we'd done some reports on jackals, so that had been seared in my brain and I couldn't stop thinking of him as one."

They had so much history together. I really felt like an outsider among them.

"It's nice to see you are still friends after so long," I said.

"We moved past friends in high school," Forrest said. "Our families were awful and we realized that family went deeper than just blood. We were a family, and we had each other's backs through everything."

That sounded amazing. I wanted that.

"Why would they decide to suddenly target me?" I asked. "The other mob I mean."

"They saw you at the office," Forrest said. "They probably did digging after that and discovered that you were dating us, and decided they would steal you and use you as a bargaining chip to get the deal they were denied earlier."

"That seems a bit extreme and stupid," I countered.

"They act first and think later," Stephan said. "Which was a huge reason I turned them down. I don't want idiots as business partners."

Wait, didn't I used to know someone with the last name of Holmes?

"Bobby. Barry. Bob. Bart," I started saying the names, trying to find the right one. It started with a B.

"What are you mumbling guys' names for?" Arcadio asked, scowling at me.

"Benjamin. Brady. Bryan. Bruce. Bruce!" I tapped Stephan's shoulder because he'd turned around. "Is one of the Holmes' Family named Bruce? Does he walk with a limp?"

His eyes narrowed at me. "Yes. Why?"

I dropped my head down and covered my face with my hands. "Oh, no." No, this couldn't be happening. I couldn't have stumbled into a similar circle as Bruce again.

"Amelia?" Stephan asked.

"One of the towns I stayed in was run by a mob. Well, I didn't know it was a mob back then. I just thought they were a gang. I suppose now it makes more sense with how they acted that they weren't a gang."

"Amelia, you're rambling," Forrest said.

"I was hired by one of their low level people to help with a robbery. We were going to steal some jewels from an old rich lady. I didn't know they'd planned on killing her. So, I stopped them. We stole the jewels and left, but they were pissed I stopped them from killing the lady because now she could report the crime and could give a description of heights and genders from our arguing. Bruce decided to pay me a visit to personally kill me, but I broke his leg and escaped."

"I thought we agreed no more secrets?" Dane asked. His hands gripped the steering wheel so tight his knuckles were white.

"There were a lot of jobs I did in all of those towns," I mumbled. "I didn't mean to hide it. I just didn't think you wanted to hear about every illegal thing I did."

Stephan rubbed his temples with his fingers and closed his eyes. "So, they might not even be after you in connection with us. They might be after you because they recognized you and Bruce wants you dead."

I shrugged. "Maybe."

"You broke his leg and he has a permanent limp," Stephan

said. "You are the only person to ever hurt him. They take that very seriously, as he is the heir to the Holmes' family fortune. If I were them, I would want to kill you, too."

I stuck my lip out in a pout. "That's not very nice."

"They still shouldn't have attacked our place and shot at us," Shea said. "They would have been smarter to try to kidnap her from the building."

"They still might try to," Stephan said. "Oh, Amelia, you are such a handful."

"I was just protecting myself. Should I have let them kill me? They were just a disorganized gang when I was there. I tried to convince them to let me go and I would leave town and never look back. He wouldn't take that and attacked me. The only reason I escaped was due to his arrogance and thinking he could kill one harmless little girl."

"I am not saying you should have let them kill you," Stephan said. "You are, however, giving me cause to negotiate with them so they don't continue trying to hurt you."

"What can we offer them?" Shea asked.

"I'll call Bryce when we get to the house," Stephan said. "I might be able to get us off lightly if I remind him how stupid and reckless Bruce is."

"If we need to pool our resources--" Dane said.

Stephan interrupted him. "Dane, you forget who I am."

"Just offering, boss," Dane said. "I'm the one who brought her into this."

"I approved it. Plus, I'm pretty sure she saved our lives with her driving and shooting skills," Stephan said. "Also, they're likely responsible for her cafe being burned down, and I can't allow that to go with no repercussions. That is in my territory and you visited it often. They're lucky I don't just consider this a war declaration."

My first day on the job and I started a mob war. That had to be a record.

"Am I going to get fired?" I asked Arcadio in a whisper.

He shook his head with a wide smile. "No."

"You're the only one I've ever met who was excited about organizing our filing," Stephan said. "I'm not firing you even if you did start a war."

"Could I just apologize and let them spank me or something?" I asked.

"No," Shea, Dane, Forrest, and Arcadio snapped.

I raised my hands in surrender. "I meant metaphorically."

"They sent newer recruits to attack the house, most likely because they wouldn't know whose house it was," Forrest said. "I guarantee the ones we let go are hiding somewhere, afraid we're going to hunt them down and kill them now that they know who we are."

"You think they told them the truth about how they were thwarted?" Arcadio asked.

Stephan chuckled. "Doubtful. Who wants to admit they were bested by a tiny, unarmed woman?"

"Bruce would believe them, though," I said with a wide smile. "They can all hate me together."

Forrest sighed and ran a hand down his face. "Honey, you aren't supposed to be happy about people hating you."

I shrugged. "They hate me for being awesome. Haters gonna hate."

Chapter Fifteen

The new house wasn't a house or a mansion. It was a plantation. Well, used to be a plantation anyway.

A large, modern security gate blocked the gravel road that lead up to it. Atop each side of the gate were rectangles that looked suspicious. "What are those hiding?" I asked.

"Turrets," Stephan answered.

The gravel road was at least half a mile long before we made it to the house.

"How did you convince the historical people to let you buy this?" I asked as we walked up the steps.

Two men in butler suits opened the front doors and rushed down to the SUV to grab the bags.

"I won this in a poker match," Stephan said.

A woman in a pastel summer dress waited inside the entry way. "A little advance notice is appreciated."

Stephan gave her a peck on the cheek and said, "You got as much notice as I could give."

"This her?" the woman asked and gave me a thorough once over.

"This is Amelia. Amelia, this is Gertrude. She runs the house when we're away," Stephan introduced.

I held out my hand. "Nice to meet you."

She shook it with a surprisingly firm grip. "Nice to meet you as well. If these boys treat you poorly, let me know and I'll knock some sense into them."

"You know we treasure women," Arcadio said, and kissed her cheek before heading towards the staircase off to the right.

"I'll show you the available rooms," Forrest said. "Follow me."

"Nice to meet you," I said again, and then jogged up the stairs after Forrest.

Once when I was in high school, we had visited a plantation house. They'd kept everything intact and decorated as it would have been three hundred years ago. Stephan and the others had opted for a different route.

"Is that room painted completely black?" I asked.

Forrest nodded. "That's the decompression room."

"The what?"

"When we're feeling too overwhelmed or just need to calm down, we go in there, shut the door, and decompress," he explained.

The next two rooms were painted pretty normally, but the furniture and bedding were completely contemporary.

"This room," Forrest said and pointed into a peach colored room with a four-poster bed that took up most of the room. He pointed into the room across from it. "This room." That room was painted white and had a small bed, a twin or full at the largest.

"Um, any others?" I asked.

He smirked, walked to the next two sets of doors and pointed at both of them simultaneously.

One was white with a small bed, just like the previous room.

The fourth room, however, was painted purple and had a king-sized bed with a low frame. I walked into the room to inspect it further. There was a single window with a tree outside it and a perfect view of the sunset over a field of flowers.

"This one," I said.

"It does suit you," Forrest said.

"Amelia?" Stephan called from the hallway.

"She's in here," Forrest said and stuck his head out of the room.

Stephan came in and smiled at me. "Is this the room you've chosen?"

I nodded. "If that's alright with you?"

"I told you that you could choose any of the available rooms. I'll have Jamison bring up your suitcase. The bedding was just washed, so you don't need to worry about it being dusty," he said.

"Thank you," I replied and rested my fingertips on the window. The view was so beautiful. I just wanted to sit and stare out at it until the sun fully set.

"Dinner will be ready in twenty minutes," he added.

"What are we having?" Forrest asked.

"No clue," Stephan replied. "Come with me for a moment, please."

I turned, but Forrest had already followed Stephan out of the room, so clearly, he hadn't meant me.

"So, you want to tell me anymore fun stories?" Dane asked as he sat on the edge of the bed.

"None really come to mind right now," I answered.

He sighed.

I sat on his lap, one leg on each side of him, and put my arms around his neck. He draped his arms around my waist and pressed his hands against my lower back, holding me in place. "I promise I didn't purposefully withhold information. If you want, I can sit with you and try to remember all the things I've done."

"Are there any other gangs, tribes, mafias, mobs, groups, or families you have pissed off?" he asked.

I shrugged. "Probably."

He dropped his head down and rested his forehead against my shoulder. "Babe—"

Threading my fingers through his hair, I ran my fingers gently up the back of his skull. "Am I giving you a headache?" I asked.

He moaned softly.

On the way back down his head, I let my fingernails scrape slightly.

His hands began to stroke up and down my back as I scraped my nails up and down his head and neck.

"You aren't a headache. My worry about your safety is giving me a headache," he replied. He slightly turned his head and kissed my neck. "I haven't even gotten to second base yet."

I snort-laughed, pulled his hands from behind me, and pushed them against my chest. "Second base has now been scored."

He rubbed his thumbs over my nipples, looked up, and covered my mouth with his. His tongue slipped into my mouth and stroked mine.

I moaned into his mouth and gripped the back of his head. My hips rocked against him and he groaned and gripped my breasts lightly.

With a gasp I pulled back and said, "The door is open."

He rolled us over, placing me on my back on the bed, stood, and kicked the door shut. "Problem solved," he said and ripped his shirt off.

Holy abs. I had known he was muscular, but I had not realized how ripped he was.

He crooked his finger at me. "Come here, beautiful."

I crawled on the bed on my hands and knees, stopping at the edge.

"Stand up," he said with a smirk.

Once I stood before him, he lifted my shirt off over my head, tossing it on top of his shirt on the floor.

Unable to stop myself, I reached out and rested my fingers on his abs.

He squatted down, picked me up under my butt, and his mouth crashed into mine as our bodies pressed together. Only my bra separated our top halves from being fully skin to skin.

I unsnapped my bra and let it fall to the ground.

His eyes lowered to my exposed breasts.

With my pointer finger, I tilted his chin up and then kissed him. Leaning forward, I wrapped myself around him so that our bare skin fully touched.

He walked forward and fell onto the bed. My back hit the mattress and he propped himself up on his arms to look down at me. "You're beautiful."

I stroked my fingers from his chest down to his abs and said, "You're not hard on the eyes either, Crackers."

His green eyes lit up, he smiled, showing off those sexy dimples, and chuckled. "You just love our nicknames, don't you?"

Instead of answering him, I knocked his arm out from under him and flipped us over so I sat atop him. "There's a lot to love with this group," I replied.

He gripped my hips and rocked beneath me. "I think there's even more to love than you've experienced."

I slid down his legs, kissing my way down his body as I did, and stopped at his pants, biting the button. "I'd love for you to share some more lovely experiences with me."

The bulge in his pants flexed. "Would you?" he asked, his voice hoarse.

I unbuttoned his pants, pulled the zipper down slowly, and tugged on the sides of his pants. "I'd like to start with you taking these off."

He kicked his shoes off and then shoved his pants down and off, raising his butt up to do so.

I stood and admired the sight of him, completely nude and hard, waiting for me.

"Yeah, I definitely won't kick you out of my bed for eating crackers," I said.

He leapt up, grabbed me, and tossed me onto the bed. I'd only had on sweatpants, so he easily yanked them off. "Good to know," he said as his mouth covered mine.

Chapter Sixteen

The week flew by as we drove from the plantation to work, worked a full eight hours, and drove back each day.

The guys had carried all of the pending filing into my office and I got to work sorting it.

Thankfully, they had a pretty decent filing system, so I didn't have to change it, and it was easy to follow along with.

Stephan let me bring a small radio into my office so I could listen to music while I organized the papers.

If it weren't for the guys coming to get me for lunch and end of shift, I might have stayed in the office organizing nonstop. When I was busy, the time flew by.

On Friday, Stephan needed to stay late, so I opted to work a bit of overtime.

I had just finished organizing the last document from one of the boxes when Forrest came into the office and shut the door behind him.

"Hey, handsome. What's up?" I asked him with a wide smile. I tossed the now empty box into the far, right corner with the others.

He leaned against my desk and said, "I feel like I haven't

really had much time alone with you, so I snuck away to come see you."

I sauntered over to him and stood up on tiptoe to kiss him. "Naughty boy."

He smirked and then looked down and asked, "Are you barefoot?"

"The heels hurt and I'm standing most of the time while I'm filing. Stephan said as long as I kept my door closed that I could remain barefooted," I explained.

Forrest chuckled. "You're just making him break all the rules, aren't you?"

"I asked first," I said and shrugged. "He could tell me no."

Forrest wrapped an arm around my waist and pulled me flush against him. "I don't think anyone could tell you no."

"So, if I asked you to make out with me right now, you wouldn't refuse?" I batted my eyelashes and stroked my finger down the middle of his chest.

He slowly turned us around, picked me up, set me to sit on my desk, and then kissed me thoroughly. When he pulled back, he said, "I definitely would not say no."

My heart hammered in my chest and I licked my lips. "What if I asked you to...do more?"

He stroked a hand down my side, his thumbs brushing my breasts, and he said, "You have to be specific with what you consider more."

"Well, you see, when a man likes a woman and—"

My explanation was interrupted with Shea opening my door. He looked at us and smirked. "Sorry to interrupt, but the boss is looking for you, Forrest."

Forrest sighed and kissed my cheek. "Sorry, honey. To be continued later."

I pouted at Shea, "Cock block."

Shea winked. "Sorry, love. Business comes first."

They shut the door as they left and I fell back on my desk with a sigh. Damn those sexy beasts.

This was no time to wallow in my misery. I had organizing to do!

I sat up, slid off the desk, adjusted my skirt, and checked the time. Five-thirty, which meant most of the other employees were long gone. Which meant I could turn my music up!

Blasting my music, I went back around the table to continue my work.

"This paper goes here. This one goes here. That one goes there. All the papers go in their proper places," I sang to myself while dancing as I put the documents on the ever-growing piles.

I spun in a circle and danced around with papers in my hands as one of my favorite songs came on.

The last time I'd heard this song was the one and only time I had gone to a dance club. That night, I danced until my feet hurt and my body was coated in sweat. None of that mattered and my smile stayed on my face until I'd fallen asleep in my car.

The song ended and I turned back to my papers, but caught movement at my door.

Shea, Forrest, Arcadio, and Dane stood in the door, watching me with wide smiles.

My face warmed and I cleared my throat. "Um, hi. How long have you been standing there?"

"Please, don't stop just because we're here," Dane said. "We were just enjoying the show."

I stuck my tongue out at him and set the papers in my hands onto their proper piles. "Are we heading home?"

"Yes," Shea answered.

My stomach grumbled and I patted it. "We'll get food when we get home." After slipping my shoes on and turning my radio off, I turned and waved at the guys. "After you, gentlemen."

"Where's your gun?" Shea asked with a scowl.

"In my drawer," I said and pointed at my desk.

All four glared.

"You're supposed to keep it on you," Forrest said. "What use is it to you if someone opens the door and shoots at you? You wouldn't be able to jump over the table and get to the desk without getting shot."

"It's too bulky," I complained. "It pulls my skirt down and I can't exactly hide it in my clothes."

They looked me up and down and Shea made a humming noise.

"We'll need to buy her a smaller gun and a holster," Arcadio said.

I walked over to the drawer, grabbed the gun, and stuck it in the purse that was only used to carry it in and out of the building. "I've got it. Let's go."

Dane draped his arm around my shoulders and pulled me against his side. "How was your day?"

"Good," I replied with a wide smile. "I finished another box."

"Only thirty to go," Forrest said with a chuckle.

"Where's Stephan?" I asked.

"In his office," Shea said. "He ordered us to get you while he finished a phone call."

We turned down the hallway and filed into Stephan's office.

He stood at his desk, phone to his ear, and a furious expression on his face. "No. That is not a fair trade. I think you need to seriously consider what it is that you're risking by allowing your son to continue his quest for revenge on a woman who bested him for being a moron."

My entire body tensed and Dane's arm tightened around me.

"I am offering you a very good deal. I will give you a day to reconsider your response," Stephan said and hung up the phone. He stared at the desk, took a few deep breaths, and then looked up at us. "Double security on the building, Shea. Arcadio, we're on war alert."

War alert?

"We need to buy her a better weapon," Forrest said.

Stephan nodded. "Call Larson and have him bring something."

"Is there anything I can do?" I asked softly. "What if we let Bruce break my leg?"

"No," Dane said, and his grip on my arm became almost painful.

"If I can think of something, I will let you know, Amelia. For now, stay with one of them at all times," Stephan said.

"Even in my office?" I asked.

"As long as you keep your gun on you, you can stay in your office by yourself. At least, for now. If they don't back down, then we might need to keep someone with you," Stephan responded.

Having to be watched for my safety was definitely going to cramp my style. Maybe it would be better if I just stayed at the house instead of working? Stephan seemed really upset, so I would bring it up later.

"Let's head out," Stephan said. "I'm starving and need to punch something."

Dane didn't release me until we got to the garage and climbed into the SUV.

No one spoke on the drive home and I couldn't think of anything to say to break the tension. Plus, it was my fault.

At the house, I climbed out and headed straight to my room. Throwing myself onto the bed, I sighed loudly and buried my face in the pillow. I had to make this right. But how? What could I possibly offer a mafia family to let me live?

I didn't have much money, and I was saving what I could for

whatever bills I needed to pay for the café burning down. I wasn't going to rebuild it. I was just going to temporarily give up on my desire to have my own business.

I didn't have any jewels, aside from the kitten necklace Shea had given me and I was *not* going to sell that.

"Whatever you're scheming about over there, stop it," Forrest said.

I turned my head to look at him leaning in my doorway. "What are you talking about?"

"You're a woman who likes to fix problems," he said. "You don't like when you can't fix things. I am certain you are trying to figure out a way to fix the Holmes Family issue. I'm telling you to stop. Stephan will work it out and if not, we will end their family."

"You say that like it would be easy," I said. "It would be easier to just give me up."

He opened his mouth and I held up my hand.

"I am not suggesting you do that. I would try to escape if you wanted to do that. I'm just saying it's not an easy thing to do."

He blew out a breath. "You're going to give me a heart attack one of these days, Amelia."

I patted the bed and he fell onto the mattress beside me, facedown, too. Slowly, I stroked his back. "It will be okay, Flowers. If you'd like, I could ask Stephan to plant some rosebushes outside my window and you could pretend I'm a secret lover that you have to jump out the window to avoid my other lover. I bet we could even get Dane to play the angry lover. It could be a fun roleplaying day."

He laughed into the blanket, his body shaking.

"Dane would just love that," Forrest mumbled.

"We'll need to figure out a sign so he doesn't bust in too

soon. If he chases you out before I've gotten mine, I'll be very irritated," I said.

Forrest's body shook harder and he turned his head to the side to gasp for air.

"What's so funny?" Dane asked from the doorway. He had changed into a pair of dark grey sweatpants and a fitted black shirt.

"We were just discussing how irritated I'd be if you didn't let me finish first," I said and smiled wide.

His brow arched.

Forrest boomed with laughter.

"We're about to start training," Dane said.

Forrest climbed off the bed and said, "I'll change and be right there."

"You need to change, too," Dane told me.

I pointed at my chest and looked around my room. "Me?"

He rolled his eyes. "No, the girl under your bed."

I narrowed my eyes. "Don't joke about that. I have nightmares about creepy women being under my bed."

"Get changed, Amelia. I'll wait right outside the door," he said.

I smirked, stood, and pulled my shirt off over my head. "You could come in and wait."

He glanced down at my bra and then met my gaze, fiery passion filling his eyes, and said, "We don't have time for that."

I stuck my lip out in a pout. "Party pooper." I turned, unclipped my bra, let it fall to the floor, and stepped over it. "Fine, I'll get changed." I shimmied out of my pants and took the final step to my dresser.

Dane groaned softly at the door.

I bent over, opened one of the drawers of my dresser, and heard the door close.

With a victorious smile, I turned around...to find the door shut and my room empty.

Dane had run away!

"Coward," I called softly through the door while I got dressed into my sports bra, sweatpants, and tank top.

I pulled my hair up in a ponytail and threw open the door.

Dane looked me over and then turned and headed for the stairs. "Come on. We're late."

"Could have been a little later," I muttered.

He didn't respond, just lead me down the stairs, down a hallway, and down another set of stairs that lead into the basement.

I paused at the top of the stairs and swallowed hard.

The basement was fully lit up, yet my brain recalled all the horror movies I had watched. At this point in a movie, the woman would walk down the stairs only for the door to slam shut, lock, and the lights to turn off. She would scream and when the lights came back on, she would be dead.

"Babe?" Dane called up from the bottom of the stairs.

"We're not going to murder you, Amelia," Shea called from somewhere in the basement.

How did he even know what I was doing?

"Nothing good ever comes from the woman going into the basement. Especially not when there are five men down there," I replied.

"I'll build you a window seat in your bedroom if you come down and practice with us," Stephan bribed me.

I raced down the stairs and flinched when the door slammed shut.

The basement was even larger than I'd thought it would be. To the right was a storage area with metal shelves holding everything from shampoo to produce. To the left, blue mats lined the floor. One entire wall was mirrors. On the far corner were several cabinets with training gloves and other things in them. Below the cabinets were free weights.

Stephan and Shea stood in the middle of the mats, watching me, with smirks on their faces. They had gloves, foot pads, and headgear on.

Forrest, Arcadio, and Dane stood against the wall, arms crossed.

"Welcome to the party," Arcadio said and smiled.

"This basement is huge," I commented.

"I'm glad you like it," Stephan said.

"Still creepy," I mumbled.

"You can take a seat or lean next to the others," Stephan instructed me. "I'll be done with Shea in a moment."

Shea rolled his eyes. "Glad to see your ego hasn't suffered at all."

Stephan swung his leg up, aiming for Shea's head.

Shea blocked it with his forearm and took a step back.

Mesmerized, I stayed standing in the open, staring as the men sparred.

Stephan's movements looked calculated, like he didn't want to move more than he had to.

Shea danced around, feinting, dodging, and punching. For such a large man, he moved rather fluidly.

"Do you have any martial arts training?" Forrest asked.

I shrugged. "Not officially. I can do a few kicks and leg sweeps. Things that I was taught."

"Dibs!" Arcadio yelled.

Stephan and Shea paused, mid-swing, and turned to look at us.

"Dibs on what?" I asked.

"Fighting you," he replied, beaming.

"That's so unfair," Dane grumbled.

"He called it," Stephan said. "It counts."

Shea panted and said, "You can go now."

Stephan rolled his eyes. "You need to do more cardio."

Shea took off his gloves and headgear. "Yeah. Yeah. Yeah. I know."

"Do you have gloves and headgear my size?" I asked.

"I'm not going to hit you, so you don't need it," Arcadio said as he stretched on the mat.

"I don't want to hurt you," I said and gave him my best smile.

"Oh! Shots fired," Dane called. "Kick his ass, Babe."

"You like bets, right? Let's make a bet. If you can knock me on my ass, I'll give you...what do you want?"

I tapped my lips as I stretched my legs. "Hm. Well, I already have two super fancy dresses. And a new diamond necklace. So, I guess I could ask for a new phone. Mine is two models older than the most recent one."

"You could have just asked me for that as a hiring bonus," Stephan said. He leaned against the wall between Dane and Forrest.

"I don't like asking for things," I said. "My phone is perfectly functional, but if I'm making bets, I might as well ask for something fancy."

"Okay. I'll get you whatever phone you want," Arcadio said. "If you can't knock me down, you have to spend the night in my room."

"What do you mean spend the night?" I asked.

"You have to stay in my room from nine o'clock until six o'clock the following morning. You have to share a bed with me, too. No sleeping on the floor," he said. "No shenanigans will take place...unless you ask me."

"Okay," I agreed, and held out my hand.

He stepped right up to me, my boobs almost touching his chest, and shook my hand.

I smiled, moved my hands up to rest on his chest, gripped, spun into him, pivoted slightly, and tossed him over my hip.

He landed on his back on the mat, eyes wide.

"Damn!" Shea said.

"That is the first time I've ever seen someone put him on his back," Stephan said.

I dusted my hands off and turned to face the others. "You guys let your guard down a lot around women."

"Clever woman," Arcadio said, and leapt up to his feet. "Alright, you won our bet. Now, show us what you've got."

I pouted. "I just showed you, though."

"Come on," Arcadio said, and bounced on the balls of his bare feet on the mats. "Show me. Prove to us that we don't need to baby you."

Oh, they still needed to baby me.

With an overly dramatic sigh, I raised my hands up to my face, set my stance, and faced him. "Fine. Just don't tease me about how horrible my form is."

Arcadio lunged at me and I sidestepped and then swung at him.

He grabbed my arm, spun me around until my back was to his chest, and whispered in my ear, "You're supposed to follow through with your punches. Not just throw your fist to the extent of your reach."

I brought my heel up, trying to kick him, but he trapped my calf between his knees.

My balance teetered and I squeaked.

"Now what are you going to do?" Arcadio asked. "Your arms are trapped and one of your legs is trapped."

Going completely slack, I let him stumble forward from my sudden deadweight.

Once he stumbled, freeing my leg, I twisted around to face him.

He still held my forearms, so I couldn't get free, but I could kick him.

I kicked his stomach, but he tensed, taking the kick without moving. "You need to weight train."

"Yeah, I'm not exactly in top physical form," I admitted. "Not that I ever have been. Surprise has always been my best weapon."

He released me and I flopped onto my back.

"You are better than I expected," Stephan said. "But it's clear you won't be able to protect yourself should someone with even half of Arcadio's skills come after you. Sorry, love, but you'll still have to keep a guard in your office when we go in."

"Okay," I said, and stood. "And to be fair, I never suggested I could protect myself from others. Just that I could shoot them."

"Yes, we'll work on that, too," Stephan said. "Not today, though. It's too dark for that. And, I don't think we have your gun yet."

"Tomorrow," Shea responded.

"Do I still have to have a guard when I get my gun?" I asked.

"Yes," all five said simultaneously.

"Alright. Alright. Geez," I said, and held my hands up in surrender.

"Dane," Arcadio called. "Spar with me?"

Dane nodded and walked over to grab headgear for himself. "I would love to."

Chapter Seventeen

Halfway through the night, a nightmare woke me. I shook beneath my blankets and stared at the unfamiliar room for a minute before remembering where I was.

Heart still pounding, I climbed out of bed and tiptoed out of my room.

The guys had rooms down a separate hallway from mine, so I hurried over and looked down the hallway. There was only one light on.

Arcadio.

I tiptoed to his door and lightly knocked.

He opened the door and frowned down at me. "What's wrong?"

"Nightmare," I whispered. "I don't want to be alone."

He stepped back, opening his door fully, and backed out of the way. "Come on in."

"Why are you still awake?" I asked as I stepped inside.

His room was painted a burnt orange and had very few decorations. His bed was only a full size, but it didn't matter too much since he wasn't that much bigger than me.

I sat on his bed and he sat beside me.

"I was drawing and didn't realize how late it was," he told me, and picked up the drawing pad on the floor.

The drawing was of a flower with long petals with swirls and diamond designs.

"It's beautiful," I said.

He closed the book and tossed it onto his desk. "Thanks. I don't draw that often, but sometimes the urge to draw is too strong to ignore."

Even though talking to him was helping, the thought of going back to my room made my heart start pounding.

"Can...can I stay here?" I asked softly.

He looked at me a moment, head tilted to the side slightly and asked, "Do you want to talk about your nightmares?"

I shook my head. "No."

He turned off his lamp and nudged my legs. "Lay down."

Obeying, I rolled over until I was on half of the bed.

He climbed in behind me, slid one arm under my pillow just above where my head was, and draped his other arm around my waist.

I moved back so he was fully spooning me and I was enveloped in his warmth.

He kissed the back of my head and whispered, "Good night."

"Good night," I whispered back.

Far too soon, Arcadio was shaking me awake. "Come on, you've got to get ready for work."

"Five more minutes," I grumbled and buried my face in the pillow.

"I gave you ten more minutes already. Don't make me yank the blanket off," he threatened.

I sighed and sat up, stretching my arms up over my head. A squeal escaped as I reached the extent of my stretch.

Arcadio jumped onto me, making me lay back down. He

pressed his body into mine and stared down at me. "You are so freaking hot."

With a hand covering my mouth, I mumbled, "I have morning breath."

He pulled my hand away and kissed me. "I don't give a shit."

I arched up my hips, pressing into him.

His hand slid from my cheek, down my side, under my butt, and he squeezed. He pulled back and said, "If you don't want to, just tell me."

I nodded vigorously. "I want to. Yes, please."

He chuckled. "I think that's the first time a woman has ever said, 'please'."

"I'm a polite person," I said with a shrug.

He pulled his shirt off over his head and I stared at the jackal tattoo on his chest. He noticed my stare and said, "It was a birthday present from Stephan when I turned twenty-one. He made me wear a blindfold to get tattooed and wouldn't let me look until it was done."

I traced it with my fingertips and said, "It's beautiful." And it was. It had to be one of the most realistic tattoos I had ever seen.

He yanked my pajama pants off and then his jeans. "I don't have time for the long and thorough session I want to give you. So, don't judge me on this performance."

I ripped my shirt off and said, "Deal."

By the time I got the shirt off, he was already buried inside of me.

One of the perks to being wet most of the time was that I didn't require much foreplay.

I moaned and then bit my bottom lip between my teeth to cut off the sound.

He groaned and said, "Please, do not quiet yourself if you

don't want to." He pulled back and then slowly slid back into me.

"Yes," I whispered and set my hands on his chest.

His phone chimed and he growled. "Dammit."

I angled my hips down, forcing him to come out of me a bit, then arched up again. "I demand at least one orgasm, Mr. Hyde."

He arched a brow. "Jackal. Not Jekyll."

I shrugged one shoulder. "Potato. Tomato."

He gripped my hips and slammed into me fast and hard, tearing a scream and an orgasm in just a handful of strokes.

"Did...did you just orgasm?" he asked. "I mean, I could feel it, but..."

My cheeks warmed. "If done properly, I tend to orgasm fast."

His eyes lit up. "Oh, beautiful, challenge accepted."

True to his word, he definitely took the challenge seriously.

After fifteen minutes and four orgasms later, he orgasmed and we rushed to get dressed and ready. He promised to get me breakfast once we got to the building because we had missed the meal with everyone else.

Stephan shook his head at us when we climbed into the SUV, but said nothing.

The others didn't say anything either, but they didn't act upset or differently, which let me relax fully.

"I heard you had another nightmare," Stephan said.

I glared at Arcadio. "Tattletale."

"Do you want to speak to a therapist?" Stephan asked. "I can find one you can meet at the building in person or I can find one that will work with you by phone if you'd prefer that."

"Therapy is expensive," I said.

"It's covered in your employee package," Stephan said.

"None of you are going to leave it alone until I talk to someone about it, are you?" I asked.

"Therapy does wonders for your mental health," Shea said. "We all have one."

"You...all have a therapist?" I asked.

They all nodded.

Dane started the SUV and headed down the long driveway. "Yes. We all meet with ours at least once a month."

"We've also brought in a marriage counselor to deal with our friendship issues from time to time," Forrest said.

So many people took their mental health for granted and so many men refused to seek out therapy due to the stigma surrounding it in our society. The fact that they all had therapists and even a group therapist made me really reevaluate them. They definitely were not like the thugs and gangs I had known before.

"Fine, I'd rather have a phone session," I conceded.

Stephan nodded from the front seat. "Okay."

"Who's assigned babysitting duty today?" I asked.

"Me," Forrest said and turned around to smile at me. "I'll let you keep your music on and won't even snicker as you dance around and organize papers."

I stuck my tongue out at him. "I can't have my music up loud until after four. So, there will be no dancing."

He pouted. "But I wanted my own private show."

I winked. "All you've got to do is ask."

"I want a private show!" Shea bellowed.

Stephan exhaled loudly. "Stop shouting. We're in a vehicle together, Ox."

Shea shrugged. "I had to beat Arcadio to the punch this time."

"I could be persuaded to do a group show, but that would require lots of presents and drinks," I said.

Stephan groaned and dropped his head forward, covering his eyes with his hand. "Wonderful, Amelia. Now they won't be able to focus on work today because they're going to be fantasizing about you dancing for them and trying to figure out what gifts to get you."

"Sorry," I said with a wide smile.

"No, you aren't," Stephan grumbled.

I laughed. "Nope."

"Please try to get some work down today, boys," Stephan said. "You can plot over gifts on breaks, lunch, and when we get home."

"Please, boss. We're professionals," Dane said. "We'll just make her start a wish list and then we can all pick from there."

"Oh, I haven't made a wish list since I was a kid," I said with wide eyes. "I love making wish lists."

"I swear, if your wish list includes things like planners and calendars..." Forrest said and shook his head.

I scowled. "What is wrong with that? I love planners and notebooks."

"It's like we have to put stipulations on everything," Shea said with a sigh.

"You are the most frustrating and amazing woman I have ever met," Arcadio grumbled.

I beamed. "Thank you."

Once at the building, we separated to our different places.

I skipped beside Forrest down the hallway towards my office.

"You're in a good mood," he said with a smirk. "Have a good morning?"

I nodded. "Yes, I did. Thank you."

"Well, my room is always open, even if I'm already asleep. Just so you know for the future," he said.

"Noted," I replied.

He pushed open the door to my office and we were immediately thrown back as a bomb exploded.

Forrest somehow wrapped his body around mine, taking the brunt of the explosion as we were smacked into the wall of the hallway, before falling to our knees.

My ears rang, my vision swam, and I felt warm liquid slide down my face. One of my arms hurt and I couldn't move it.

People moved all around me, but I couldn't do anything.

Someone picked me up and I checked to make sure it was someone I knew.

Dane.

His lips were moving, but I couldn't hear anything.

My body felt like it was spinning and I fainted.

"I don't care! Find out where they went and bring them in," Stephan shouted.

"So loud," I whispered.

"Amelia, I'm sorry," he said, lowering his voice to a whisper. "Can you open your eyes?"

I tried, but couldn't. "No."

"One second. You have crusty stuff on your eyes."

I heard the sound of water dripping and then a warm wet cloth gently rubbed my eyes. After he dried them with another cloth, I opened them slowly.

"Hi," Stephan said. His hair was sticking up at weird angles, his shirt was rumpled, jacket missing, and his tie was loose and hanging low.

"Hi. What did I miss?" I asked. The memory of the explosion surfaced. "Oh, no. Is Forrest okay? Please tell me he's okay."

"He's okay. He is still in the hospital, too, but he's not in critical condition," Stephan answered.

I looked down at my body and realized my arm was in a cast. "What happened?"

Stephan sighed and ran a hand through his hair, making it stick up more. "Someone planted a bomb in your office. Forrest triggered it when he opened the door."

"Forrest wrapped himself around me to protect me," I recalled.

Stephan nodded. "He shielded you from most of the blast, but you did break your arm."

"What about him?" I asked, and had to clear my throat because it was dry.

Stephan grabbed a glass of water with a straw from the side table and handed it to me. "Small sips. Don't drink too much."

I obeyed despite wanting to chug the water.

"He has a concussion and several cuts, also lots of bruising, but nothing else. You were both very lucky."

"Did anyone else get hurt?" I asked. There weren't people in the offices right next to mine, but the others weren't too far away.

Stephan shook his head. "Whoever it was that planted the bomb only made one that destroyed your room and the door."

"You...you don't know who did it?" That surprised me. With all the security we had at the building, how could someone sneak in a bomb?

Stephan sat on the edge of my bed and said, "We're still investigating it. Someone used two of our employees' badges to get in through the garage access. The fact that security didn't notice their face masks is most troubling to me. We are trying to find those two employees as well. Either they were paid a lot of money and are hiding, or they're in danger."

"How come you're in here?" I asked. Immediately, I realized how rude that sounded. "I appreciate you being in here, I just would have expected you to be in Forrest's room."

He chuckled and patted my leg. "It's alright. I know what you meant. The guys have been in your room since you were brought in. Even Forrest came in here. I had to order them all out to get some food and a change of clothes. They only left when I promised to stay here with you."

They'd stayed with me, even Forrest, while I'd been unconscious?

"Why are you crying?" Stephan asked. "Are you in pain? Do I need to call the nurse—"

"I'm sorry. It's just...no one's stayed in the hospital with me before." I sniffled and tried to wipe my eyes, but the one arm was in a cast and hurt to move and the other had an IV in the back of it.

Stephan wiped my face for me. "Well, you won't have to worry about that ever again."

"Stephan, be honest with me. Why did you let me in so easily?"

He sighed and dropped his hands into his lap. "Once Dane and Forrest started to show interest in you, I ran a check on you. Not a true background check like I ran when you started, or one that accessed your felony record, though now I realize that's definitely something I need to do. This check was to see if you had any affiliation with my rivals or anyone that could potentially hurt us. It's interesting that my investigator failed to find your association with the Holmes Family, though. I will have to discuss that with them. I also hired a private investigator to follow you for a week to see if you were hiding anything. Or to see if you were an undercover cop."

My mouth dropped. He'd had me followed? For a week?

He chuckled. "Don't look so shocked, Amelia. My family is very important to me. Had I been notified sooner that you were having financial troubles with your café, I would have offered you assistance. Though, it seems like you don't have too much interest in opening back up."

"Honestly, it was a lot of work and I thought it would be rewarding, but it was too stressful. I hated fighting with the suppliers and dealing with hiring and firing employees. Is it wrong that I'm not really that upset anymore that it's gone? Like, I didn't want it to burn down, but I don't really want to try to reopen it anytime soon."

He nodded. "Dealing with employees and suppliers is never fun."

"So, do you run an investigation on any girl that the guys show a slight interest in?" I asked.

"No. I ran it once I discovered they were sneaking to your café without telling me."

"They...what?" They were so close and didn't lie to each other. Why would they hide that they were coming to get coffee and tea from me?

"Apparently, they didn't want Shea and Arcadio horning in on their time with you," Stephan explained. "Though, once they found out, Shea and Arcadio started looking you up, too. They all knew that in the end they wanted one woman to share. Don't ask me why, I don't understand the desire most people feel to be in a relationship. But that's what they want. The hounded Forrest and Dane to bring you over so they could meet you, but none of us realized that all this time, they hadn't made a move on you yet."

"I had no idea they were interested in me until Dane asked me on a date," I admitted. "I've always been a bit dense when it comes to realizing a man is interested in me, though."

"Did you have anything else you wanted to ask me while the boys are away?" Stephan asked.

"If you can confirm this came from the Holmes Family, can't you argue they broke one of my bones so we're now square?"

His eyes widened. "That's brilliant. Why didn't I think of that? As soon as I can blame them for it, I will use that."

"Who else could it be?" I asked.

The pain meds were starting to wear off and I cringed.

"Let me get the doctor," Stephan said. He stood, walked to the door, poked his head out, and waved his hand at someone.

A doctor and nurse were instantly in my room, checking my vitals and shining lights into my eyes.

They asked me questions, gave me a dose of pain meds, then pulled Stephan outside of the room to talk to him.

I wanted to see Forrest, but I didn't want to get yelled at for walking around when I wasn't supposed to.

Stephan came back in smiling. "They said you'll be able to go home today."

"What about Forrest?" I asked.

"He has to stay for the night," he answered.

"I don't want to leave him here," I said. "Can I sleep on his couch? Or can they just move my bed into his room or something?"

Stephan sighed. "You're as troublesome as those men. Let me see what I can work out. Stay in your bed unless you need to use the restroom."

I saluted him. "Yes, sir." The IV line got snagged on the bedrail and I hissed in pain. Thankfully, it didn't come out.

He sighed again, shook his head, and walked out.

I closed my eyes and exhaled. The pain was gone, but the extra weight on my arm bugged me, even with it lying on the bed.

The fact that someone had tried to blow me up in Stephan's

building, was surprising. Not that they tried to kill me, but that this was twice now they had attacked one of Stephan's places.

Were the Holmes' Family really stupid enough to think they would get away with it?

When the door opened again, I opened my eyes, and found someone I didn't know. The man was big, like Shea, wore a suit, and had dark sunglasses on.

"Who are you?" I asked, sitting up in the bed.

"If you want to live, you're going to stay quiet and follow me out of here," he said in a menacing tone.

"I've got an IV in my hand, dude. I'm not ripping it out," I said calmly despite my heart hammering in my chest. The heart monitor gave it away, beeping louder and faster.

He pulled his jacket to the side to show me the gun in a holster on his side. "We can do this the hard way or the easy way. The easy way, you stay alive. The hard way, I end you right here."

"How am I supposed to leave with the IV bag?" I asked and arched a brow.

I was really proud of the bravado I was pulling off. No clue where it came from, but I loved it.

He gritted his teeth together, lips apart. "Dammit, woman. Just get up, grab the IV stand, and follow me."

I shrugged. "Okay, but they're not going to let us out of the building." Slowly, I slid out of bed, grabbed the stand the IV bag was hooked to, which had wheels, and stood on weak legs.

As I stood, I realized I had just disobeyed Stephan's order. Would he be pissed or would he understand? He seemed to forgive me for a lot more than he did the guys, so it would probably be okay. Especially if I explained it was this or I was shot.

The guy stepped back and held the door open.

With one step, I remembered I had a hospital gown on and my butt was totally exposed.

I squeaked, grabbed the back, and pulled it slightly around to hold onto it at the same time I held the IV stand. "I don't want to flash people," I explained when the guy looked back at me.

I didn't need to see his eyes to know he'd rolled them at me.

He walked down the hallway and I followed, searching for one of my guys.

Where the hell were they? Where the hell was Stephan?

"Ma'am, you shouldn't be out of bed," a nurse called out.

"Keep walking," the man ordered me.

Despite wanting to do something, I just obeyed. I didn't want anyone else getting hurt because of me. I didn't want someone dying because I screamed or notified them.

We made it to the elevator and he mashed the button. The doors slid open and he stepped in.

I stepped forward, debating if I could force him to go down without me, but he grabbed my arm and dragged me inside. I turned around to face the hallway, looking at my open door and the man scanning the area for me.

Arcadio's eyes met mine, he looked over my head, his eyes narrowed, and he sprinted down the hallway towards us.

The guy mashed the buttons as the doors closed and we began a slow descent.

"This is probably the slowest elevator I've ever been in," I commented. "And there isn't even decent elevator music. One out of ten, would not recommend."

"Shut up," the man snapped.

When the elevator doors opened, he grabbed my arm again and dragged me down the hallway, towards the sliding glass doors that lead outside.

"Excuse me. Excuse me! She can't go outside with an IV in," a nurse called out behind us.

Where was security? There were usually security guards

209

near the exits. Was it break time? Had they paid them to be scarce?

We got to the doors, but the IV stand's wheels got caught on the tracks.

I tugged, trying to get them over, but only two of the four wheels made it.

"For fuck's sake," the man muttered. He grabbed the stand and picked it up high enough the wheels made it over. He set it down once we were clear and blew out a breath.

"Which way, kidnapper?" I asked.

"Left," he ordered me in a gruff bark.

I turned on my heel and started that way. "Yes, sir, kidnapper sir."

"Shut up," he growled. "How do they stand you? God you're annoying."

"Quirky. I'm quirky," I said.

We walked by the side of the building, towards a parking lot in the back that was almost always empty. As we passed the doorway, Arcadio leapt out of the darkness and tackled the kidnapper.

I stepped back, chewing on my lip nervously as he and the man grappled.

Arcadio pulled a knife out of his jacket and stabbed it into the kidnapper's shoulder.

The kidnapper bellowed and tried to headbutt Arcadio, but Arcadio moved faster than the big man. The kidnapper drew his gun, but Arcadio kicked it away.

Arcadio moved behind the kidnapper, wrapped him up in a chokehold, and squeezed. He gritted his teeth, his lips pulled up in a snarl as he choked him. "You thought you could just steal my girl? Who do you work for? Who?"

The kidnapper punched Arcadio, but Arcadio kept his grip.

"Who do you work for?" Arcadio demanded.

The kidnapper's face was bright red, turning purple.

"Um, Arcadio, I don't think he can answer when you're cutting off his airflow and bloodflow," I said.

"Monstress, just let me work, okay?" Arcadio said.

"Monstress?" I asked. "That's rude."

The kidnapper ripped the knife out of his shoulder and slashed at Arcadio, cutting his cheek.

I started to move forward, but then the kidnapper finally succumbed to the choking and fell face first on the ground.

Blood dripped from Arcadio's face to the ground, bright red.

"Arcadio," I gasped. "Is it bad? We're at a hospital, so we can just rush you inside."

A car swerved into the parking lot, almost hitting Arcadio and the unconscious kidnapper.

Arcadio jumped back, but not in time to avoid the guy who got out and slammed the butt of his gun into Arcadio's skull.

I screamed his name and moved towards him.

Another guy got out of the car, unhooked the IV bag from the stand, grabbed me, and climbed back into the car.

I beat on him with my one good fist, but he didn't let go.

Screaming as loud as I could, I hoped someone at least came out and helped Arcadio.

The driver tore out of the parking lot, and out onto the main road.

I stopped screaming, looked around the car at the suited and dark-sunglass-wearing men, and realized I was totally screwed.

Chapter Eighteen

My kidnappers drove me through a vineyard to a huge mansion. Outside of the mansion was a giant water fountain. The fountain sculpture was a woman with large breasts, holding her breasts around the nipples with water spraying out of the nipples in four different spots.

I scoffed and said in a deep voice, "Calm your tits." I added in a high-pitched voice, "No!"

The men looked at me, at each other, and then shook their heads.

"Don't tell me you didn't think that when you saw it, too," I mumbled.

"Carry your bag," one of the men said, and set the bag of fluids in my lap.

"Chivalry is dead," I said, and climbed out behind the man. I stood, but then had to set my bag on the seat to grab the back of my hospital gown so I could hold it and the bag at the same time.

"Hurry up," one of the men snapped.

I mimicked him silently and followed them up to the mansion.

They held the door open for me and I walked into a foyer decorated in deep burgundy with the lights on low.

"Welcome to the haunted mansion," I whispered in a deep voice.

Normally, I wasn't so snarky and outspoken. I blamed it on the drugs.

The men herded me down the hallway, into a large room where Bruce and an older version of Bruce sat at a table with glasses full of red liquid.

I rolled my eyes. "Is this where one of you tells me you're really vampires and invite me to join your coven?" I asked.

"I told you she was insufferable," Bruce said.

"Oh, look at you using five dollar words." I smiled sweetly at him.

"You don't realize the trouble you're in," older Bruce said.

"Look, man, I am hopped up on pain meds, wearing a hospital gown, and holding a bag of fluids that I'm supposed to have hanging beside me. Either you are going to kill me or you're going to use me as a bargaining chip against the Moriarty Family. Either way, I have no say. I can't kill you with my IV cord. I can't drown you in the fluids inside this bag. I'm just a woman with a busted arm who is here against her will. So, I can either go out crying and asking for mercy. Or, I can be a smart ass and enjoy my last hours on earth."

"Can someone gag her already?" Bruce asked with a sigh.

"Can I pee first?" I asked, and shifted on my feet. "I haven't been able to go since I became conscious."

"How did you survive the bomb?" older Bruce asked.

"I didn't go into the office. Forrest opened the door and it activated the bomb and he shielded me with his body," I explained.

"Take her to the restroom," older Bruce ordered someone behind me.

They lead me down the hallway to a restroom, but made me keep the door open.

I set my bag on the counter, held my gown, and peed. I had underestimated how badly I needed to pee. The pee was probably the longest I had ever had.

Once done, I felt much better. I washed my hand, grabbed my fluids bag, and followed the kidnapper back to the room.

Older Bruce waved at one of the seats.

I thought he wanted me to sit at the table, but instead, one of the men dragged a chair back, pushed on my shoulder to force me to sit down, and then they tied my arms and legs to the chair and put a piece of duct tape over my mouth.

They did at least hang the fluids bag on the high back of the chair so it would work properly.

Older Bruce took a picture of me and then started furiously typing on his phone.

Not even a minute later, his phone rang.

He answered with a smug smile. "Hello, Moriarty." He listened and his smile wilted. "I think you fail to understand the situation you are in. I have your woman and if you don't do as I say, I will kill her."

He listened a bit longer and I watched as the color drained from his face.

What was Stephan saying to him? Dammit, I hoped someone was recording this.

"You have one hour to bring me two million dollars, or I will kill her," Older Bruce said.

Even from where I was, I could hear Stephan's laughter.

Uh oh.

"You think this is funny? I've got your little bitch here, in my house, and at my mercy," Older Bruce snapped. His eyes raised to mine and I gave him a small smile.

Shit.

"One hour, Moriarty," Older Bruce snapped and hung up the phone. He set it on the table and exhaled. "That asshole."

How could I get myself out of this one? How?

I couldn't even talk.

Well, that might have been to my benefit, honestly.

"What did he say?" Bruce asked.

"In one hour, if he isn't here with my money, we're going to cut one of her fingers off and send it to him," Older Bruce said.

I closed my eyes so he wouldn't see me roll my eyes. Such a cliché thing to do. Really? My finger?

"Go check the perimeter," Bruce ordered the guy behind me.

The door opened and closed behind me.

Bruce walked over to me, limping on the leg I had broken. "Do you know how much shit I got for this limp?" he asked me.

I shrugged.

"They mocked me for being bested by a woman. I killed over a dozen men after you injured me," he said.

He walked over and stood before me, fury in his eyes. "You fucking bitch."

I couldn't say anything, so I just rolled my eyes dramatically.

He drew his hand back and slapped me across the face.

My head whipped to the side and my vision blurred a moment.

Wow, that hurt. A lot.

There was a loud thud outside that drew his attention.

Had my legs not been tied to the chair, I would have kicked him in the shin.

"Check it out," Older Bruce ordered him.

The door opened and Bruce backed up, his mouth open wide.

"I always knew you were stupid, but I didn't realize you were so stupid that you thought you would survive attacking one of my family and blowing up a room in my building," Stephan said behind me.

I closed my eyes and tears built in them. He'd come.

"Do you have my money?" Older Bruce asked.

Stephan stopped beside my chair and set his hand on the back of it. "It's a good thing you didn't take a new wife or have any more children. I hate killing innocents."

"Where's my money?" Older Bruce asked again, and stood.

"Hey, Monstress," Arcadio whispered as he squatted beside me and started cutting the ropes from my arms and legs. "I'm sorry they got you." He had a wide bandage on his cheek, hiding the wound he'd gotten from the first kidnapper's knife.

Stephan walked forward and stood across the table from Older Bruce. "You knew she was part of my family. You knew that my men loved her. Yet, you still thought you could hurt her and get away with it. It's time you were put down."

Older Bruce smirked. "You don't kill people, Moriarty. You're too soft."

Stephan drew a handgun from his jacket and shot Older Bruce between the eyes. He turned and shot Bruce in the head, too.

If my mouth hadn't been taped, it would have dropped open.

"We need to get her back to the hospital," Arcadio said. "Her complexion is even paler."

Stephan turned and scowled. "What's with the wide eyes, Amelia?"

Arcadio ripped the tape from my mouth and I hissed in pain.

"You killed them," I responded after a moment. "You don't kill people."

He put his gun in its holster and folded his arms over his

chest. "They hurt you and Arcadio. They needed to die and I didn't have anyone close to do it. So, it was up to me."

"Is she safe?" Shea asked behind me.

Arcadio stood and nodded. "Yes."

"He was so mad when you laughed at him," I told Stephan. He smirked. "I'm sure he was."

"I thought you might leave me," I admitted.

Arcadio picked me up in a bridal carry and shook his head. "Even if Stephan had left you, I would have come for you."

"Me, too," Shea said.

"I am going to choose to ignore that they just admitted they would commit insubordination," Stephan said. "I was not going to leave you. I just had to bluff a bit so I could make it in here without him realizing I was so close."

"We followed you within a minute of them taking you," Shea said. "We tossed Arcadio into the SUV and followed."

"I'm really sorry," Arcadio whispered.

I reached out, but paused just a hair away from touching the bandage on his cheek. "I'm sorry you got hurt."

"It's going to make a cool scar and you'll just have to kiss it every time it hurts," he said.

"Come on, let's get her back to the hospital," Stephan said and walked out of the room.

"Thank you, for coming for me," I whispered.

Arcadio pressed his lips to my forehead and said, "We will always come for you. You are ours."

"Always," Shea said with a nod from the doorway.

218

As soon as I got to the hospital, Forrest and Dane rushed into my room and refused to leave.

After the doctor gave me a thorough examination and removed my IV, he placed me on a day of bedrest at home.

He left like his pants were on fire, shutting the door behind him and trapping me inside with five scowling men.

"Why didn't you yell for me?" Forrest asked. "I was right next door."

"He had a gun," I reminded him.

"So, did I," he countered.

"Oh," I replied. I had not known that. "But he said he would shoot me if I screamed. I didn't want to get shot."

"Why didn't you alert the staff?" Dane asked.

"I didn't want him to shoot anyone," I said. "I didn't want anyone else to get hurt."

"Forrest's injuries are not your fault," Stephan said softly, his voice gentle.

"He called me annoying."

Dane chuckled. "I'm sorry, Honey. We don't think you're annoying."

"So, am I forgiven?" I asked.

"You disobeyed my direct order," Stephan said, before the others could respond.

I flinched. "I was hoping you wouldn't remember that."

"So, in punishment, you have to spend two days at home, in bed, only getting up to use the restroom. All of your meals will be brought to you. You will not have your cell phone or any books to read, either," he said sternly.

My mouth dropped open. "That is cruel and unusual punishment! You can't take books away from me."

"You disobeyed me. I can punish you as I wish," he said, and shrugged.

Arguing would probably just extend my punishment, so I just puffed my cheeks in annoyance.

"We forgive you," Shea said.

"Um, did you call people to clean up...you know?" I asked Stephan.

He smirked. "Yes. Don't worry, all traces of you are gone. No one will know you were involved in any way, and the five of us are clear as well."

"Did you confirm they were the ones behind the bomb?" I asked.

Forrest nodded. "Yes. And we found out that they were also behind your café burning down."

My mouth dropped. "Seriously? That's just rude."

"They were also behind your slow business," Dane added. "They threatened the security company and suppliers, and spread lies about the café so business would be low."

I closed my eyes and blew out a breath. "All because I broke his leg so he couldn't kill me. What a putz."

Stephan tried to hold in his laughter, making a "pfft" sound. Then, he let it out.

I opened my eyes to scowl at him, but seeing him doubled over, clutching his stomach as he laughed, made my scowl disappear.

Soon, the others joined his laughter.

For once, I didn't mind being laughed at.

Dive into UNINTENTIONAL PIRATE to find out what happens next for Amelia and the Moriarty Mafia.

The Story Continues

If you enjoyed this novel, be sure to check out book two in the series:

UNINTENTIONAL PIRATE

About the Author

Daisy Emory is the contemporary romance and contemporary reverse harem romance pseudonym for USA Today Bestselling Author Catherine Banks.

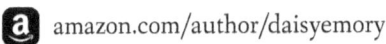 amazon.com/author/daisyemory

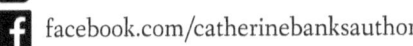 facebook.com/catherinebanksauthor

www.ingramcontent.com/pod-product-compliance
Lightning Source LLC
Chambersburg PA
CBHW021244260626
47155CB00004BA/1306